TALES OF REAL
ESCAPE

Paul Dowswell

Designed by Mary Cartwright
and Nigel Reece

Illustrated by Peter Ross and Tony Jackson

Additional illustrations by Janos Marffy
and Sean Wilkinson

Editorial assistance by Lisa Miles

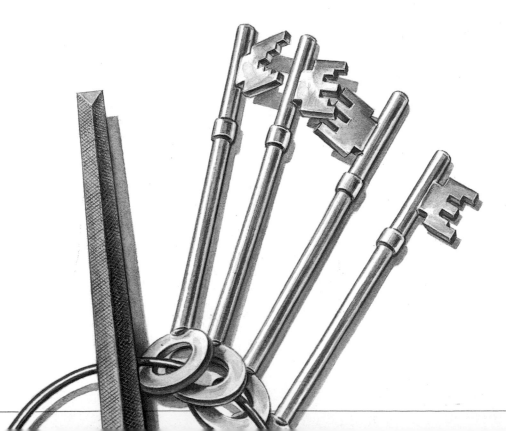

Contents

Escapers at work 3

Snakes and sharks guard jungle prison 4
Harrowing tales from the penal colony of French Guiana.

Churchill's track to fame and freedom 10
Journalist Winston Churchill's Boer War breakout.

Alcatraz accordionists break out of the Rock 12
Did three convicts survive the freezing waters of San Francisco Bay
to beat this "escape-proof" prison?

Ivan Bagerov – Royal Bulgarian Navy 18
Will David James's Bulgarian disguise fool every soldier and policeman he meets?

Knitting needle escape for Soviet master spy 22
George Blake's audacious getaway from Wormwood Scrubs prison in London.

Plüschow's dockland disguise 26
Vaseline, boot polish and soot transform debonair Gunter Plüschow.

Harry Houdini – escaping for a living 30
Escapologist Harry Houdini claimed that no lock, handcuff or prison in the world could hold him.

Colditz Castle – escape-proof? 34
The German prisoner of war camp held 800 of the most determined escapers in Europe.

Harriet "Moses" Tubman leads slaves to freedom 40
A former slave helps other slaves escape in pre-Civil War America.

Escape or death for Devigny 44
Will a pin, razor blade and spoon save André Devigny from a firing squad?

Breakout at Pretoria Prison 46
Three men create a key for every door between their cells and the entrance of Pretoria Prison.

Mountain-top escape for Italian dictator 52
Commando Otto Skorzeny comes to the rescue of dictator Benito Mussolini.

Berlin – the prison city 54
Ingenious, desperate and dangerous escapes from East Berlin.

Escape films – fact or fantasy? 60
A guide to films based on stories in this book.

After the escape 62
Celebrity, wealth, infamy or anonymity. What happened to the people and places in this book?

Further reading, acknowledgements and index 64

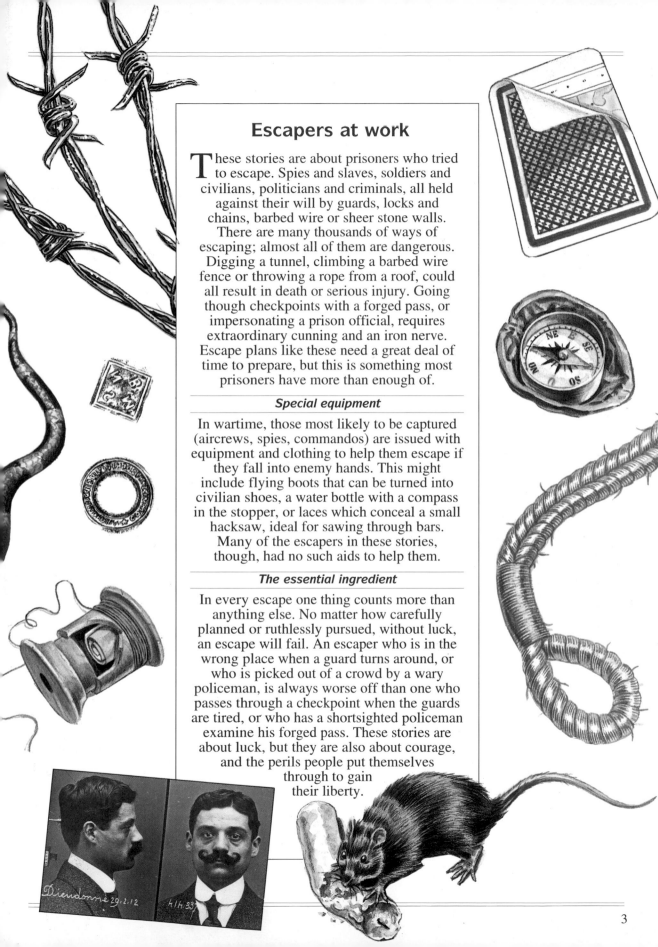

Escapers at work

These stories are about prisoners who tried to escape. Spies and slaves, soldiers and civilians, politicians and criminals, all held against their will by guards, locks and chains, barbed wire or sheer stone walls.

There are many thousands of ways of escaping; almost all of them are dangerous. Digging a tunnel, climbing a barbed wire fence or throwing a rope from a roof, could all result in death or serious injury. Going though checkpoints with a forged pass, or impersonating a prison official, requires extraordinary cunning and an iron nerve. Escape plans like these need a great deal of time to prepare, but this is something most prisoners have more than enough of.

Special equipment

In wartime, those most likely to be captured (aircrews, spies, commandos) are issued with equipment and clothing to help them escape if they fall into enemy hands. This might include flying boots that can be turned into civilian shoes, a water bottle with a compass in the stopper, or laces which conceal a small hacksaw, ideal for sawing through bars.

Many of the escapers in these stories, though, had no such aids to help them.

The essential ingredient

In every escape one thing counts more than anything else. No matter how carefully planned or ruthlessly pursued, without luck, an escape will fail. An escaper who is in the wrong place when a guard turns around, or who is picked out of a crowd by a wary policeman, is always worse off than one who passes through a checkpoint when the guards are tired, or who has a shortsighted policeman examine his forged pass. These stories are about luck, but they are also about courage, and the perils people put themselves through to gain their liberty.

Snakes and sharks guard jungle prison

Herded off the steamship *Martinière* at gunpoint, around 600 shaven-headed convicts lined up on the quay of St. Laurent, deep in the jungle of French Guiana. A random collection of thieves, swindlers, thugs and murderers, all had been sentenced by French courts to exile or imprisonment in this remote and inhospitable South American colony.

The *Martinière* sailed twice a year from France and those on board endured a diabolic 18 day journey. Packed 90 a time in cages and fed from buckets, they were hosed down with seawater every morning. Not everyone survived the voyage.

Exhaustion and disease

Nothing these men had seen in Paris, Marseilles, or a hundred other provincial towns had prepared them for St. Laurent. The hot, sticky air carried a forewarning of exhaustion and disease. Emerald vegetation beyond the town and river banks concealed a dense, dark world, infested by insect legions and poisonous snakes. From time to time strange birds broke cover, shimmering by in a blaze of reds, greens and blues.

A ragbag crowd

Everybody in St. Laurent stood staring by the quay. The ship's arrival was the main event of the year. Chinese shopkeepers, Guianan bushmen, the wives and children of the guards, and prison officials in spotless white suits, all gazed with curiosity as the *Martinière* disgorged its bedraggled human cargo.

Most convicts boarding the *Martinière* (top) never saw France again. Their journey, sketched above by a fellow convict, was a harrowing one.

Two French Guianan convicts, 1938. Their tattoos are typical of the prison colony population.

Creatures such as this poisonous coral snake inhabited the jungle around the prison camps.

Painful memories

Scattered among the crowd were a handful of pitiful, dead-eyed men, whose ragged clothes hung loose on ravaged, tattooed bodies. The *Martinière* stirred up painful memories for them. They too had arrived in this way, perhaps decades before. A life of hellish brutality, disease and degredation lay behind them. Now they waited for death to release them. Any new arrival who saw these embittered figures would have shuddered. If they survived, this would be their future. Many convicts faced a life sentence, but even those with limited time to serve would probably spend the rest of their life there. The law required them to remain as residents for a period equal to their original sentence.

A veteran of 20 years of prison colony life. 1930s.

The penal colony of French Guiana

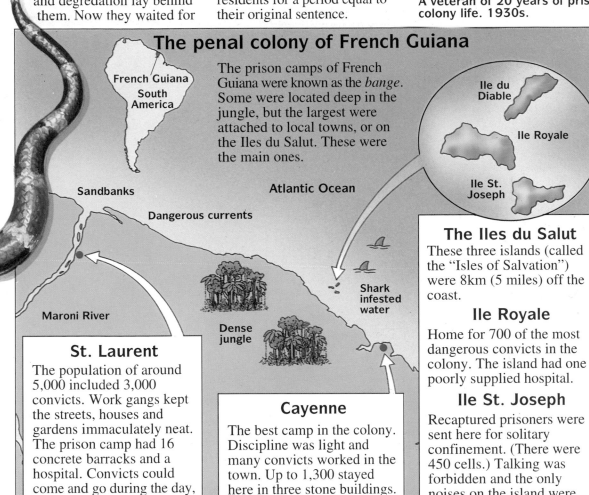

French Guiana **South America**

The prison camps of French Guiana were known as the *bange*. Some were located deep in the jungle, but the largest were attached to local towns, or on the Iles du Salut. These were the main ones.

Ile du Diable

Ile Royale

Ile St. Joseph

Sandbanks

Atlantic Ocean

Dangerous currents

Shark infested water

Maroni River

Dense jungle

The Iles du Salut

These three islands (called the "Isles of Salvation") were 8km (5 miles) off the coast.

Ile Royale

Home for 700 of the most dangerous convicts in the colony. The island had one poorly supplied hospital.

Ile St. Joseph

Recaptured prisoners were sent here for solitary confinement. (There were 450 cells.) Talking was forbidden and the only noises on the island were the cries of those driven insane by their seclusion.

Ile du Diable

Political prisoners were sent here. This former leper colony was the smallest of the three islands and known throughout the world as "Devil's Island". Around 30 prisoners lived here, at any one time.

St. Laurent

The population of around 5,000 included 3,000 convicts. Work gangs kept the streets, houses and gardens immaculately neat. The prison camp had 16 concrete barracks and a hospital. Convicts could come and go during the day, but had to be back in the camp at night.

Cayenne

The best camp in the colony. Discipline was light and many convicts worked in the town. Up to 1,300 stayed here in three stone buildings.

A dreadful warning

Near the quay stood the prison gates, where the unnerved arrivals were greeted by the prison director. He made the same speech to all newcomers.

"You are all worthless criminals, sent here to pay for your crimes. If you behave yourselves you'll find life is not too unbearable. If you don't behave, you'll find yourself in more trouble than you can begin to imagine.

Most of you here are already thinking about your escape – forget it! You will have plenty of freedom in your camps and in town. You'll find that the real guards here are the jungle and the sea."

But life was unbearable. Men spent exhausting days toiling in jungle work gangs, tormented by insects, and supervised by guards who had the power of life or death over them.

Worse than villains

These guards were often more corrupt than their prisoners. The French Emperor Napoleon III set up the prison camps in 1854, to rid France of its worst criminals and help revive an ailing, under-developed overseas colony. He was asked by an aide:

"Who, Sire, will you find to guard these villains?"

He replied:

"People more villainous than they are."

Napoleon III was as good as his word. Tales of torture, sudden execution, and burial alive, perpetrated by guards such as "Tiger" Bonini, or "The Scourge" Alari, filtered back to civilization.

These guards reported their victims as having "died from the effects of a fit" and convicts would do anything to avoid falling into their clutches. Members of a work gang supervised by Bonini were said to have hanged themselves with jungle creepers, rather than spend another day working for him. Others deliberately infected themselves with tuberculosis or leprosy, risking death or disfigurement to avoid the jungle work parties.

17,508 hours alone. Solitary confinement on St. Joseph

The guillotine was the most severe punishment a convict in French Guiana could expect. Almost as bad were the solitary confinement cells on the island of St. Joseph. Here men could be sent to spend up to five years alone, and four out of five went insane or died.

Solitary confinement cell

Iron bars

Hinged plank bed

Chamber pot

Iron door

Hatch

The cells were stark, and inmates were given barely enough food to keep them alive. In the cell blocks all was silent. Prisoners were forbidden to talk. The guards even wore slippers to cut down on noise.

Papillon

Some did survive though. One famous description of these cells comes from the book *Papillon* by Henri Charrière. He was sentenced to French Guiana in 1931 for murder – a crime he claimed he did not commit. Many people believe this book about his life as a convict is only partly true, but its account of solitary confinement is thought to be realistic.

Cigarettes and coconuts

Charrière, who spent two years in solitary confinement following an unsuccessful escape attempt, stayed healthy for most of the time.

Feeding time in the cells, depicted by a convict artist.

Friends arranged for five cigarettes and a coconut to be smuggled to him every day. The coconut supplemented his poor diet and the cigarettes enabled him to break the monotony of his day.

Chasing centipedes

He kept sane by passing secret messages to other prisoners and chasing centipedes. Most of the time he led a rich fantasy life, dreaming about girls, countries

Night-time feuds

Night offered no relief. Convicts were locked into huge prison camp dormitories – the scene of interminable fighting between feuding gangs. Here men were terrorized into giving up their last meagre possessions or silently murdered in the stale, stinking dark.

50,000 escapes

Despite the prison director's warning, most convicts did try to leave the colony. Life was so bad that the punishment for escaping, two or more years of solitary confinement, was not a sufficient deterrent. 70,000 men were sent here between 1854 and 1937, and over 50,000 escape attempts were recorded.

It was not difficult to slip away from the camps or work gangs, and roll calls were only held twice a day. Getting out of the jungle was the hard part.

An uncertain fate

Only one in six escapers avoided recapture, and it is impossible to say how many of these actually got away. Many nearby countries returned convicts to their captors, so those who fled kept quiet about their past.

Most men probably paid for an escape with their lives. The director's warning about the jungle and the sea was not a bluff. Rough seas and strong currents overturned flimsy boats, leaving their occupants to drown.

Men escaping by land fell victim to poisonous snakes. Others found themselves hopelessly lost in the dense jungle, and died starving and alone. Insects ate their bodies, leaving no trace.

Safety in numbers?

Convicts almost always escaped in groups, as the perils they faced were too great to cope with alone. However, ruthless men, hardened by years of captivity, do not always make the best travel companions.

The Longuevilles

In one incident in the 1920s, brothers Marcel and Dedé Longueville escaped with four other convicts. The Longuevilles, huge, tattooed thugs, were two of the most terrifying convicts in the colony. Three of the other escapers contributed money toward the cost of a boat. The fourth did not. He claimed to be an experienced sailor and his skill paid for his place on the trip.

The six men left St. Laurent one December night, planning to sail their well-equipped boat down the Maroni River and on to Cuba. A strong current carried them under the noses of the guards and out to sea.

But here their troubles began. The estuary where the Maroni meets the Atlantic Ocean has sandbanks which stretch for miles along the coast.

No sooner had they taken to sea than the boat became stuck on such a sandbank. Dedé Longueville, overcome by a towering rage, stabbed the sailor to death.

Stranded

The remaining five waded ashore. A large wave washed away their supplies so they had to look for food in the jungle. There were only small crabs to eat, and after a few days they were starving. Two of the party, a tough Parisian villain named Pascal and his young companion, were sent into the jungle to search for food.

The next morning Pascal returned alone, and told them he had lost his friend. Although the Longuevilles would kill a man who let them down, they would not desert a fellow convict. They took Pascal back into the jungle to look for his companion.

A terrible discovery

Inland, they made a terrible discovery. Pascal had killed his friend and eaten parts of his body. The Longuevilles were filled with disgust and killed him on the spot. However, later that night their hunger overcame their scruples. Pascal himself was eaten and the grisly evidence was discreetly buried.

A few days later the men were recaptured by the local police. They returned to French Guiana to spend two years in solitary confinement.

---

he had visited, and his childhood.

One year and nine months into his sentence, his daily supply of coconuts and cigarettes was discovered and stopped. Without his extra rations and the distraction of cigarettes, his health and sanity declined rapidly. Fortunately, he had only three more months to go. After 17,508 hours of isolation he was released, and sent back into the penal colony.

Henri Charrière, during his trial in 1931.

The Guianese assassin

A few years earlier, other runaways had also faced an unpleasant fate. Some local colonists could be bribed to help convicts escape, but others, such as fisherman Victor Bixier des Ages, would take a bribe and then kill a man for the rest of his money.

Bixier des Ages agreed to take parties of five or six to Brazil on his boat. A day into the voyage he would sail through sandbanks and ask passengers to step out, so the boat could float over the shallow water. As they stood up to their knees in the muddy bank, he would reach for his gun and shoot them dead.

Cold-blooded murder

No one knows how many died this way, but eventually Bixier des Ages grew careless. On one occasion, as he dispatched a party of five escapers, he ran out of ammunition. One man managed to wade to the shore and evade his executioner in dense jungle.

This man survived to be recaptured, and told the prison authorities his tale. The fisherman was arrested and sentenced to 20 years on Ile Royale, where all native French Guianese were sent. Even here he continued to bring grief to the convicts of the colony. He became a turnkey, a trusted prisoner whose job it was to track down escapers.

A trip to Brazil

Some convicts did survive to reach other countries. Eugene Dieudonné made three attempts before he succeeded. One time he fled with two others, on a raft made from ladders lashed to barrels. They spent two days surrounded by sharks, their legs dangling between the ladder rungs. Although they were not attacked, their nerve gave out and they returned to captivity, and a spell in the solitary confinement cells on Ile St. Joseph.

Drowned in mud

Dieudonné finally escaped from the colony in 1927, this time with five others. They bribed a fisherman to take them in his boat, but were soon stranded on coastal mudbanks. Although the boat was refloated it sank in heavy seas a day later. The escape party managed to swim to the shore, but one, a young

Police photograph of Eugene Dieudonné. 1912.

man named Venet, sank up to his shoulders in the muddy slime of the seashore. His companions attempted to reach him with branches torn from trees, but Venet drowned when the tide returned.

Jungle hideaway

The party split into two groups, with Dieudonné pairing up with a Breton named Jean-Marie. The other couple were soon recaptured but Dieudonné and the Breton hid in the forest for a month, paying two old convicts to supply them with food. These convicts also put them in touch with a reputable sailor, known as "Strong Devil", who agreed to take them to Brazil.

They sailed with three other fugitives in an open fishing boat which had to be constantly bailed out. The voyage drained the strength from the already exhausted escapers, but "Strong Devil" lived up to his name. He navigated the boat through heavy seas and they reached the Brazilian coast after seven days. Slipping past the local police they headed inland to the town of Belem, where they hoped to find work.

Carnival tramps

With great good fortune the escapers arrived during the annual carnival, and revellers assumed they were dressed for the occasion as carnival tramps. Dieudonné and Jean-Marie set about making a fresh start. They gave themselves new identities, found a room to rent, and lived a quiet respectable life. Dieudonné worked as a cabinet maker and Jean-Marie assisted him. But the past caught up with them. After four months the two were betrayed, and arrested by the local police.

Famous convicts

However, Dieudonné was a famous man. He had been part of a notorious terrorist gang in France. After the gang was arrested, four of them were guillotined, but Dieudonné, who was only a minor member of the gang, was sent to French Guiana. At the time, many people felt his sentence was too harsh. The Brazilians decided they were not going to send a possibly innocent man back to the horrors of French Guiana.

Jean-Marie had no such luck. His past was not so interesting and he was sent back to the penal colony, but Dieudonné became the focus of an international press campaign, and the French government was persuaded to pardon him. Not only had he escaped from the penal colony, but he was able to return to France as a free man.

Endless terror

Others returned to France too, but as escaped, unforgiven criminals. They led shadowy lives, forever in fear of an unexpected knock on their door. They could be arrested at any time, and have to go through the awful voyage on board the *Martinière*, two years of solitary confinement, and more endless years in the jungle of French Guiana. More often than not they were betrayed by an acquaintance, or even a member of their own family.

A French journalist known to be sympathetic to the plight of these fugitives, once received a letter from such a man, whose wife and child knew nothing of his former life as a convict.

Sometimes I start to shake when someone stops too long at my stairwell, or each time there are voices from the other side of my door.

When he wrote the words above he had been on the run for 22 years.

Where they went – escape destinations

The most practical way out of French Guiana was by sea. Convicts escaped in a variety of vessels, from cobbled together ladders and barrels, to dug-out canoes and small fishing boats.

For those who survived their journey out of the colony there were plenty of destinations to head for, although wherever a convict went, he faced an uncertain future.

Vessels used by escapers.

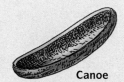
Canoe

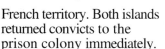
Barrels and ladders

Fishing boat

British Guiana

Escapers were not welcome here, nor in any other British territory. Most convicts were permitted to head for other countries, rather than returned to French Guiana.

Martinique and Guadaloupe

French territory. Both islands returned convicts to the prison colony immediately.

Venezuela

Convicts were accepted here and work was available. However, in 1935 the army hired a French convict to assassinate president Juan Vincente Gomez. He failed. In the reprisals that followed, all former French convicts were rounded up and returned to the prison colony.

Trinidad

Trinidad declared in 1933 that it would help escapers. It became too popular a destination, so began to send runaways on to other countries.

Dutch Surinam

Until 1924, this was the best place to go. All but the worst convicts were allowed to stay here, and work was easy to find. However, in 1924, a drunken escaper burned down a shop when he was refused service, killing the owner and his family. After this, all convicts were sent straight back to French Guiana.

Brazil

Escapers were usually sent back, but Brazil is so big many of them were able to hide from the authorities.

Argentina

It was difficult to reach from French Guiana, but there was plenty of work for seasoned criminals in Buenos Aires – the crime capital of South America.

Churchill's track to fame and freedom

Winston Churchill, journalist for the London *Morning Post*, crouched low outside the high wall of a Pretoria school where he had been held captive. He had leapt over, as a guard beneath turned to light his pipe. Now he had been waiting 15 minutes for two other prisoners to follow him. People were passing by. The guard stood a breath away.

The school had been turned into a prisoner of war camp during the Boer War. The Boers (descendants of Dutch settlers) had rebelled against British rule in South Africa in 1899, and set up their own territory.

Churchill had been captured by Boers when they ambushed his train. He had put up such a fight that they refused to believe he was a journalist and held him prisoner with British troops. Now, hidden only by a small bush, he was in terrible trouble. His fellow escapers were obviously not going to join him, but his journey to British territory depended on them. They had money, maps and a compass, and one spoke Dutch – a language understood by his captors. He could not go back, because the wall outside the school was too high to climb.

Bold gamble

Churchill had no choice but to escape alone. As he wore civilian clothes he decided he might not be noticed. He stood up slowly and walked straight past a sentry by the main gate of the school. He walked down the town's main street toward the station, nervously whistling to himself. A railway line ran between Pretoria and the

Winston Churchill in 1899.

port of Lourenço Marques (now named Maputo) which was in neutral territory, so he decided to hide on a train.

Railway getaway

Churchill lay in wait outside Pretoria Station. With great risk to his life he boarded a train by climbing up onto the couplings between two wagons. The train he had chosen was full of

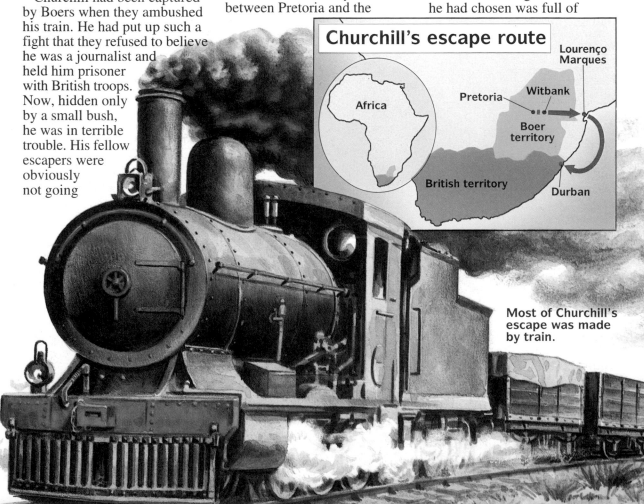

Churchill's escape route

Africa

Pretoria
Witbank
Lourenço Marques
Boer territory
British territory
Durban

Most of Churchill's escape was made by train.

empty coal bags, and it trundled slowly through the night to Witbank, a small mining town 95km (60 miles) east of Pretoria.

As dawn broke, Churchill feared he would be seen. Leaping from the train he hid in a forest, intending to board another train that evening. In the undergrowth he lay so still that a vulture, thinking he was dying, kept him company. By dusk Churchill was beginning to feel very hungry, so he made his way to some nearby lights, which turned out to be a town.

Held at gunpoint

Knocking on the door of a house, he was greeted by a man who pointed a pistol at him. Churchill told him he was "Doctor Bentinck" and that he had fallen off a train and lost his way. This unlikely story was unconvincing, so Churchill told him the truth.

Fortunately his captor, John Howard, was English. Howard told him that this was the only house in 30km (20 miles) where he would not have been arrested.

Dead or alive

By now Churchill's escape had been featured in the British newspapers and the Boers were anxious to find him. They were offering a £25 reward for the Englishman "dead or alive", so Howard decided to hide his fugitive in the town mine.

Churchill spent three dark days in a pit pony stable infested with rats, who soon ate his supply of candles. In such grim surroundings he became ill, and was taken to the surface and hidden in a store room.

Howard had a friend, Charles Burnham, who came to their

While Churchill hid in a mine, rats ate his candles.

rescue. He hid Churchill in a delivery of wool he was sending by train to the coast. The journey passed without incident, but at the border Churchill had to endure an 18 hour wait. The train was searched, but he was too well concealed to be discovered.

Hero's welcome

When the train arrived at Lourenço Marques, Churchill immediately boarded a boat to the British territory in South Africa. At the port of Durban he was greeted by an excited crowd. Already quite well known as a journalist, his escape had turned him into a national hero.

On his return, Churchill joined the British forces in South Africa to fight his former captors. He also continued to work as a journalist, and his fame enabled him to become the highest paid war correspondent of his day.

These pictures of Churchill's escape appeared in a London magazine.

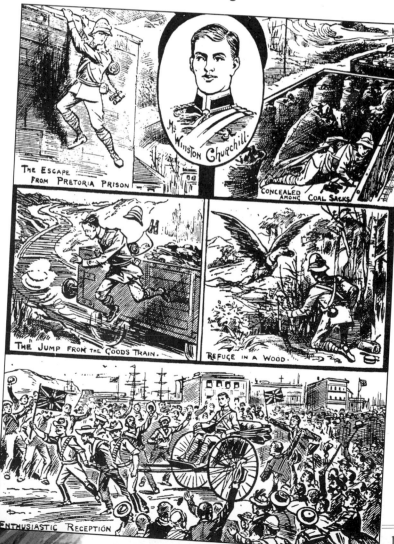

THE ESCAPE FROM PRETORIA PRISON

Mr Winston Churchill.

CONCEALED AMONG COAL SACKS

THE JUMP FROM THE GOODS TRAIN.

REFUGE IN A WOOD.

ENTHUSIASTIC RECEPTION

Alcatraz accordionists break out of the Rock

The long corridors of cellblock B were buzzing. Behind steel bar doors, convicts called out chess moves to nearby opponents. Others swapped jibes and threats, or washed and undressed for the night. Activity ceased abruptly at half past nine, when the lights were switched off.

Frank Morris, bank robber and burglar, stared at the ceiling, alone in his cell. His world measured three paces by five. Day one of his ten year sentence on "the Rock" – Alcatraz Top Security Island Penitentiary – was over. All around him were men regarded as the most hardened, desperate criminals in the entire USA. The Rock was their ultimate escape-proof punishment.

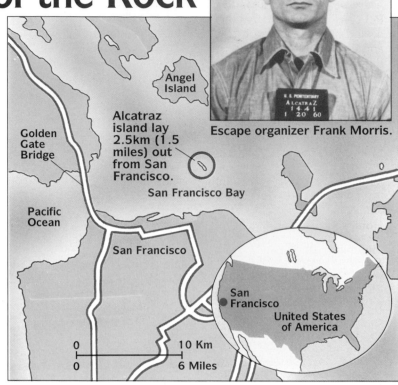

Angel Island

Alcatraz island lay 2.5km (1.5 miles) out from San Francisco.

Golden Gate Bridge

San Francisco Bay

Pacific Ocean

San Francisco

Escape organizer Frank Morris.

San Francisco

United States of America

0   10 Km

0   6 Miles

Foghorns and footsteps

The stillness beyond was broken only by the distant boom of a foghorn and the footsteps of a patrolling guard. In the cavernous steel and concrete block the sound of each step took a second to settle. Morris noted the time it took the guard to walk the length of a corridor before he turned around. Already he was planning his escape.

260 closely packed men

In the dead of night all that remained to remind Morris of his fellow inmates was the dark, brooding smell of 260 closely packed men and a high, sharp whiff of disinfectant. It unsettled him at first, but after a few days there he would no longer notice.

Outside, the winter wind stirred. Howling across San Francisco Bay, it tugged at the jagged island fortress, and lashed the cold, dark sea. The wind rose and fell, seeping through windows and doors, penetrating the cell blocks, stairwells and galleries of the prison.

Razor sharp

Morris's pleasant face and amiable manner hid a ruthless determination and razor sharp mind. Escaping was in his blood. His mother Clara escaped from home aged 11, a school for wayward girls at 14, and a reformatory at 17. Morris was born, and abandoned, shortly after.

A childhood of foster parents and children's homes followed, and a career in burglary. A series of prison sentences, escapes and recaptures, led him to Alcatraz.

Rock routine

As the days went by he became accustomed to the routine of the Rock: the daily workshop visit to earn money making brushes or gloves; the journey back to the cells through a metal detector; random body searches and half-hourly head counts; two afternoon hours' recreation in the yard; three meals in the prison canteen, with its ominous riot precautions – rifle slits in the wall and silver tear gas bombs nestling in the ceiling.

After the evening meal the men were locked in their cells. They had four hours to themselves before the lights went out, to paint, read, or play a musical instrument. Then they settled down to a long dreary night which dissolved into the harsh wake-up blast of the 6:00am horn.

Alcatraz – the island of pelicans

In 1775 Spanish explorers named the island *Isla de Alcatraces* – "the Isle of Pelicans", after the birds that nested on it. In 1850 a fort and lighthouse were built there. The army used the island as a disciplinary barracks, and between 1906-1911 they built the prison that still stands today.

Alcatraz became notorious when many of the infamous gangsters of the 1930s were sent there. "Creepy" Karpis, "Machine Gun" Kelly and Al Capone were all residents. Its reputation for impregnability and harshness was deliberately encouraged by an American government intent on discouraging lawbreakers.

Al Capone, top gangster and Alcatraz resident.

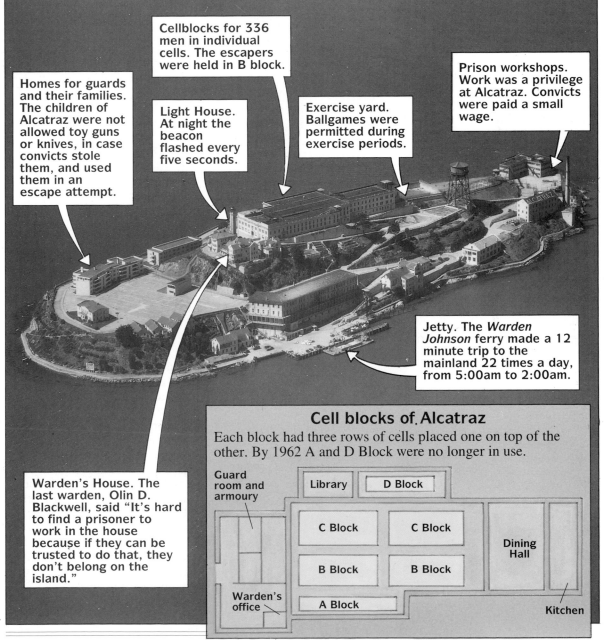

Cellblocks for 336 men in individual cells. The escapers were held in B block.

Prison workshops. Work was a privilege at Alcatraz. Convicts were paid a small wage.

Homes for guards and their families. The children of Alcatraz were not allowed toy guns or knives, in case convicts stole them, and used them in an escape attempt.

Light House. At night the beacon flashed every five seconds.

Exercise yard. Ballgames were permitted during exercise periods.

Jetty. The *Warden Johnson* ferry made a 12 minute trip to the mainland 22 times a day, from 5:00am to 2:00am.

Warden's House. The last warden, Olin D. Blackwell, said "It's hard to find a prisoner to work in the house because if they can be trusted to do that, they don't belong on the island."

Cell blocks of Alcatraz

Each block had three rows of cells placed one on top of the other. By 1962 A and D Block were no longer in use.

Guard room and armoury

Library   D Block

C Block   C Block

B Block   B Block

Dining Hall

Warden's office

A Block

Kitchen

Fellow felons

Morris soon got to know his fellow felons. In the cell next door was Allen West, an accordion-playing New York car thief. Unlike the quiet Morris, West was full of boundless conversation.

In the canteen Morris met the Anglin brothers, John and Clarence – burly Florida farm hands, bank robbers and hardened prison veterans. Their cells were on the same level, farther down the corridor.

A way out ?

In conversation with another prisoner, Morris learned that three years before, a large fan motor was removed from a rooftop ventilator shaft above his block. It was never replaced. His sharp mind instantly envisaged a daring night-time getaway through the shaft. There was a way out of impregnable Alcatraz, just 9m (30ft) above his head.

Bank robber brothers John (left) and Clarence Anglin.

Inspiration strikes

Morris began to plot. It seemed impossible to reach the shaft from a locked cell, but one day inspiration struck.

A small air vent sat just below his sink. Beyond it lay a narrow utility corridor carrying water, electricity and sewer pipes. If Morris could take out the vent and make a hole big enough to crawl through, he could climb up to the rooftop ventilator shaft and out onto the roof. He picked at the

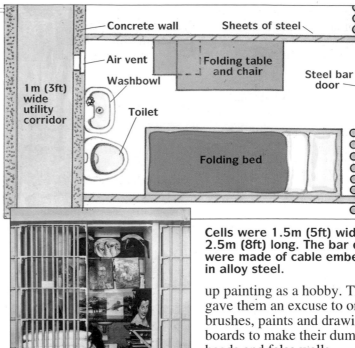

Cells were 1.5m (5ft) wide and 2.5m (8ft) long. The bar doors were made of cable embedded in alloy steel.

concrete around the vent with nail clippers. Tiny flakes fell at his feet.

Hiding the hole would be difficult, but not impossible. An accordion like West's would be big enough to cover the early excavations. He ordered one, paying with money earned in the glove workshop.

A fake wall

Then he hit on the idea of making a false section of wall, complete with painted air vent. A dummy head could be made too, from papier-mâché, to place in his bed while he was away from the cell. The more he plotted, the more he realized this plan would work better with others to escape with him.

Escape committee

West and the Anglin brothers were recruited. Their close proximity in the cell block would be useful. The four became an escape committee. Their first move was to all take

up painting as a hobby. This gave them an excuse to order brushes, paints and drawing boards to make their dummy heads and false walls.

First steps

While West watched for patrolling guards from his adjoining cell, Morris began to dig away at the air vent with a nail clipper. After a slow hour he had collected a small pile of fragments.

Work stopped before lights-out, debris was cleaned away and the accordion placed over the evening's work. Morris's fingers ached. The nail clipper would take months to dig through the concrete.

A new tool

The team met next morning at breakfast. The Anglins had been digging too, and had found it tough going. A more solid tool was needed. Their breakfast spoons were good and heavy – perhaps they could be put to use?

Morris slipped his into a pocket, and that night he prepared his cell for some ingenious improvised metalwork. He broke the handle off the stolen spoon and removed the blade from his nail clippers. With this, he shaved slivers of silver from a dime. Then, he tied fifty or so matches into a tight bundle.

Morris intended to melt the silver to solder the blade to the spoon handle. The blade and handle were held in place above the matches with piles of books, and silver scraps were sprinkled between them. The matches were lit and a fierce heat welded silver, blade and handle together.

The new tool made digging less tiring, but even so, it was still not strong enough to hack through 20cm (8in) of concrete. Even greater ingenuity was needed.

West to the rescue

Making use of his job as a prison cleaner, West managed to steal a vacuum cleaner motor, and with parts pilfered from the prison workshop, he was able to turn it into a makeshift drill.

It was extremely noisy, and could only be used during the prison music hour, when inmates were allowed to play their instruments. So great was the risk of discovery that the escapers only used the drill to make the initial holes in their walls, and continued to chip away at the walls at night with their digging tools.

Drawing board wall

Work also began on the false walls, which would be made from drawing boards. They were painted the same shade as the cell wall, and an air vent was added.

When completed they were placed over the holes in the real walls which were chipped away to the same size. In bright light the fake walls would not survive a second glance, but in the dim recess of a cell they blended in well enough. Taking turns keeping watch, the escapers drilled and chipped at

their walls day after day. Eventually they made holes large enough to squeeze through.

Dummy heads

Next, pages from magazines were torn up, and soaked in the cell sinks. The soggy paper was mashed up into a pulp to make papier-mâché, and fashioned into the shape of four dummy heads. A few nights later the heads were dry enough to paint.

Clarence Anglin, who worked as a prison barber, added an authentic touch. He supplied his fellow escapers with plenty of hair, which was glued onto the scalps and eyebrows of the dummies. These they intended to leave poking out of their bedclothes while they were absent from their cells.

Trip to the top

When the heads were finished, Morris took a trip to the roof. He placed his dummy head in the bed and squeezed through into the utility corridor. It was dark and damp and smelled of the seawater that flowed through the sewage pipes. He climbed up a pipe through the tangle of conduits, mesh, wiring and catwalks, and reached the roof ventilator shaft. It hung down 1.5m (5ft) from the ceiling and took a sharp right angle 30cm (1ft) inside.

A spoon, nail clipper, matches and a silver dime were used to make digging tools.

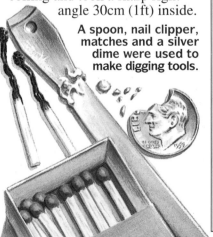

Vacuum cleaner drill

Here is how a vacuum cleaner motor was used to drill holes in the cell walls.

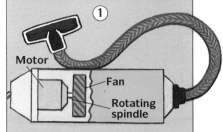

Vacuum cleaners have a motor which turns a fan to suck air into the cleaner.

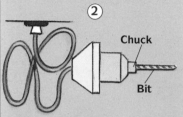

The motor from the cleaner, and a drill chuck and bit stolen from the prison workshop, were attached to the spindle. (The motor was plugged into a light socket in the cell.)

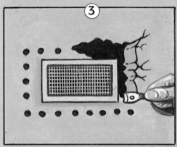

Holes drilled around air vent. Concrete scooped out with a digging tool.

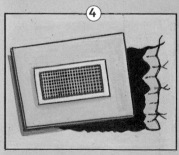

A false wall made from art class drawing board was placed over the hole.

Morris would need someone to help lift him inside. He also noted that there was ample space near the shaft to store material for the swim to the mainland, 2.5km (1.5 miles) away. The escapers planned to make water wings, or even a raft, from plastic raincoat sleeves. Filled with air, these would provide buoyancy in the numbing waters of the bay.

Stealing plastic raincoats was easy. A large pile was freely available near the basement workshop. John Anglin wore a new one every day on the way back to his cell.

Escape route blocked

Morris made another trip to the roof. Clarence Anglin came too, to help him into the shaft. What he saw inside filled him with misery. Although the fan blade and motor were no longer there, the top of the vent was still blocked by two bars,

An accordion was large enough to conceal a hole in the wall.

a grille and a rain hood. All were firmly anchored in position by solid steel rivets.

A new plan

Over the next few days Morris mulled over this setback. The two bars could be bent back with a length of pipe left in the utility corridor, but the rivet-held grille and hood were far more of a problem. The vacuum cleaner drill would have been handy, but the noise it would make in the still of the night made it impossible to use.

Carborundum string, a thin cord, coated in abrasive powder, was suggested. It was used to saw through metal in intricate repair work in the prison workshops. It would mean many more evenings of extra work, but this was the only way to remove the rivets. The cord was duly stolen.

By mid-summer of 1962, six months after the first digging began, the rivets were finally detached. The escapers replaced them with rivet-shaped balls of soap, which they painted black. They did not want a guard to peer into the shaft and notice the rivets were missing.

Time to go

Now nothing stood in their way. All they needed was to agree on a date. The Anglins pressed to go at once. Morris, ever cautious, wanted to research tides and currents in the treacherous water of the bay, so they agreed to wait for ten days.

The ventilator shaft rivets were removed with cord coated with abrasive powder.

But their anxiety was growing. Up in the ceiling a pile of sleeves and sleeveless raincoats awaited discovery.

Cell search

That week cells were being searched at random. Both Anglin brothers returned from meals to find subtle changes – a towel moved here, a book moved there. West was yet to be visited, but he worried incessantly about his fake wall, which kept slipping. There was a bag of cement in the tunnel, so he decided to patch up the fake wall until the night of the escape.

Premature departure

Seven days before the agreed date, the Anglins could wait no longer. Around nine o'clock on the evening of June 11, Morris heard a voice behind his fake wall. John Anglin was telling him they were going NOW. Before Morris could argue, Anglin was off up the corridor. Next door, West was panic-stricken. Unprepared, he began chipping at the hardened cement seal around his fake wall, choking with anger and frustration.

West deserted

Morris kept watch for West. For now, the bustle of the cell block's evening activities muffled West's frantic digging. But soon the lights would go out, and silence would fall on the block. Morris could wait no longer. He left the desperate West and climbed the pipe to the roof where the

Anglins were waiting. All agreed on the need for silence – whispers only, no banging. Noise travels farther at night.

A dangerous mistake?

Squeezing into the shaft, Morris removed the soap rivet heads, his face starkly lit by the recurrent flash of the lighthouse beacon. The grille was gently eased from its moorings and handed down. But as the rain hood was lifted away, a gust of wind seized it, and it clattered noisily to the roof. Morris felt his muscles tense to near paralysis.

Below, the noise was noted by a patrolling guard. He consulted an officer. They were not too concerned. It could be a bucket, or an empty can of paint. There was plenty of loose junk to blow around in the wind.

Out on the roof

Five minutes passed before Morris emerged onto the roof, blinking at the dazzling beacon. The Anglins followed.

The route from rooftop to island shore passed by brightly floodlit areas, overlooked by gun towers. They could wait for a sea fog to settle on the island, or move immediately and risk being spotted. They moved onward.

Hugging the shadows, they crawled to the edge of the roof. Below was a 15m (50ft) drop. Morris lowered himself over the rim and onto the pipe with infinite slowness, lest a sudden movement catch the eye of a guard, and slid down the floodlit wall with the same deliberation. Reaching the bottom of the pipe without being seen, he crawled over to the safety of the shadows at the other end of the block. The others followed.

Into the ocean

They made their way over a succession of small barriers – a cyclone fence here, a barbed wire fence there – and down a shallow cliff to the seashore.

The mainland beckoned. Crouching in damp sand, the three inflated their raincoat water wings, then waded through a sharp wind into the dark, freezing waters of San Francisco Bay.

Empty beds

At daybreak guards sent to wake the missing men found only dummy heads in their empty beds. Other prison officers recalled the noise that roused their suspicions the night before. They estimated the escapers must have entered the water around 10:00pm, when the bay was calm, and the currents advantageous. If they survived the cold they had every chance of reaching the mainland.

Boats, planes, soldiers and dogs were sent out to find them. Two days later a plastic bag was recovered from the bay. Inside were sixty family-album photographs, addresses and a receipt belonging to Clarence Anglin.

After that, nothing. No bodies. No clothing. No sightings. No trace. The three could have been washed out to sea and drowned. But it was equally likely that they escaped. Whether they are still alive, or met an early death in the criminal underworld they no doubt returned to, no one knows.

As for West, he finally chipped away his false wall after midnight. He shinned up to the roof but Morris and the Anglins were long gone. Poking his head through the ventilator, he disturbed a flock of seagulls. They made such a screeching cacophony that he panicked, and fled back to his cell.

He spent the rest of his sentence wondering what would have happened if the Anglins had given fair warning of the escape. Maybe he'd be in a quiet backwater bar, with a long cool drink and a beautiful girl. Maybe he'd be lying at the bottom of the Pacific Ocean, his bleached bones picked clean by crabs.

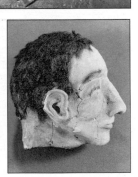

Right. A day after the breakout a guard inspects the hole and fake wall in the utility corridor behind the escapers' cells.

Below. The dummy heads used by Morris and the Anglin brothers in this escape can still be seen on display at the National Maritime Museum in San Francisco.

Ivan Bagerov – Royal Bulgarian Navy

Lieutenant Ivan Bagerov of the Royal Bulgarian Navy would present a benign, if slightly puzzling figure, to the minor officials he would encounter on his travels around northern Germany. He spoke almost no German, and carried a collection of Bulgarian documents that would be quite incomprehensible to the average policeman, guard, or railway ticket inspector.

At least that was what Bagerov hoped. He was really Lieutenant David James, of the British Royal Navy, and he was about to escape from the German prisoner of war camp of Marlag und Milag Nord, near Bremen. The year was 1943.

Ingenious outfit

His disguise, and the props that accompanied it, were ingenious. As a foreigner who spoke almost no German, he thought he would be most convincing posing as another foreigner. He decided he would be a naval officer, because his own uniform was a naval one.

Bulgaria was one of Germany's allies during the Second World War. James thought few people would know what their naval uniform looked like, especially as the Bulgarian navy was very small.

British Navy brass buttons.

Bulgarian Navy shoulder insignia.

To add credibility to this disguise, he sewed a gold and blue insignia to the shoulder of his uniform. On this, in the letters of the Bulgarian alphabet, were the initials KBVMF, which stood for Royal Bulgarian Navy.

A flimsy cover

Bulgaria was also a monarchy, like Britain, so this would explain the crowns on the brass buttons on James's naval uniform. James was gambling on the fact that no one he met would see though this flimsy disguise and recognize his British naval uniform.

The forged Bulgarian identity papers he carried were another asset. Every day, policemen and soldiers checked the papers of German civilians, or Dutch or French workers. They would probably have never seen a Bulgarian document before, and would be less likely to spot a forgery.

Pure fiction

The identity card was pure fiction. No one in his prisoner of war camp had any idea what this should look like. James had no photograph of himself, so a magazine picture of a German naval captain was used. The face was obscured by a fake Bulgarian stamp.

Once he reached friendly territory he would need to prove he really was David James. Rather than carry his real identity papers in his case, where they could be found by a curious soldier or policeman, he sewed them into the lining of his uniform. James made sure that everything in his suitcase looked Bulgarian. He even scraped the brand name

James's fictitious Bulgarian Navy identity card used a photograph taken from a magazine.

off his soap, and replaced it with a Bulgarian letter. Labels for his clothes were more difficult to change. Two Greek officers gave him their tailors' labels. The Greek lettering was nothing like the Bulgarian alphabet, but at least it was different from the British words on James's labels.

Love letters from a ballerina

Also in the case were several love letters, written in a Russian hand (which uses the same alphabet as Bulgaria), and a photograph of glamorous English ballet dancer Margot Fonteyn. James intended to tell anyone searching his luggage that Fonteyn was his Bulgarian fiancée. The picture would, he hoped, divert their attention.

A bogus letter of introduction to show to any suspicious official was also concocted by a friend in the camp. This was vague enough to explain his presence at any port he might be able to reach, and also excused his poor knowledge of German.

Almost everything in James's case was faked, or modified to make it look Bulgarian.

The letter read: "Lieutenant Bagerov is engaged in liaison duties of a technical nature which involve him in much travel. Since he speaks very little German, the usual benevolent assistance of all German officials is confidently solicited on his behalf."

Major setback

James planned to travel to the nearby city of Bremen were he could take a train to the coast. Unfortunately, just as he was about to begin his escape, a group of British naval prisoners from the camp were taken to Bremen for medical treatment. This meant that local people would know for certain what British naval uniforms looked like, and James's thin disguise would be even more risky.

Danish disguise

This problem was solved by modifying his uniform yet again. He would travel to Bremen dressed as a Danish workman, and take on his Bulgarian disguise at the station. James set about inventing a character for himself. He would become Christof Lindholm, a Danish electrician who was spending a few days in the countryside.

The brass buttons on his jacket were covered with black silk, and a cloth cap was made out of a pocket lining. A check scarf and grey flannel trousers completed the outfit.

Grave doubts

On the day of the escape, December 8, 1943, he began to have grave doubts. It was a horrible cold morning, there was a nice warm fire in his room, and besides, he was acutely nervous. But as so many fellow prisoners had helped him prepare for the escape, he felt he could not let them down.

The escape begins

Getting out of the prison camp was easy. James climbed out of a shower room window in a building right on the perimeter. Walking away in his disguise, he could have been any local workman.

Half way up the road away from the camp, James faced his first test. He was stopped and questioned by the local policeman. This man was suspicious and looked in his case. Fortunately James had had the foresight to hide his Bulgarian documents. They were strapped to his leg with sticking plaster. All the policeman could see were clothes, but still he was uncertain.

Roadside interrogation

The questioning began. Where was he staying? Who was he staying with? The first thought that came into James's head was that the local priest was looking after him. He did not know his name, and told the policeman he just referred to him as "Father". Thinking desperately, he tried to flesh out his story. He was staying in a church. The priest was an older man with grey hair. These rather obvious details were still not enough to convince his interrogator.

A fortunate forgery

However, James had another trick up his sleeve – a forged letter from the local hospital, telling him to report there that afternoon. This finally convinced the policeman, who sent the escaper on his way, and he reached Bremen station without further incident. Once there, he went into the station lavatory and changed into his Bulgarian naval officer's uniform, stuffing cap and trousers behind a water pipe. As a final touch he darkened his light hair and moustache with theatrical make-up, to try and make himself look convincingly eastern European.

Beer and tickets

Back on the platform he was stopped by a guard. James handed over his letter of introduction and was presently provided with an assistant. This man bought him a ticket to the port of Lübeck, found out which train he should take, and then took him to the waiting room and ordered him a beer.

The train arrived and James headed for the coast. Wherever he presented the fake Bulgarian pass, it was accepted without question, even though the only intelligible thing on it was a photo of someone else, and a serial number.

Changing trains at Hamburg, James went to the station restaurant to eat. Here he was eyed suspiciously by a German soldier sitting at his table. Fearful that the man could recognize his British uniform, James stared back defiantly, and embarrassed the soldier enough to make him turn away.

That night he spent an uncomfortable few hours in a waiting room in Bad Kleinen. He had covered almost 320km (200 miles) in a single day.

Noisy Nazis

Next day he continued on to the Baltic port of Stettin, sharing a compartment with several noisy Nazi soldiers. Here he got off and searched the town's docks for a Swedish ship. Sweden was a neutral country, and if the ship's crew could be persuaded to take him out of Germany, he could travel back to England from Sweden. But there were no Swedish ships in Stettin, so James consoled himself by visiting several of the town's bars, where he kept his ears open for any Swedish voices.

Lucky Lübeck?

He took the train to the port of Lübeck, breaking his journey overnight at Neu-Brandenburg to sleep at the *Wehrmachtsunterkunft* (a military rest camp similar to the YMCA). Again James felt extremely anxious that his uniform would be recognized.

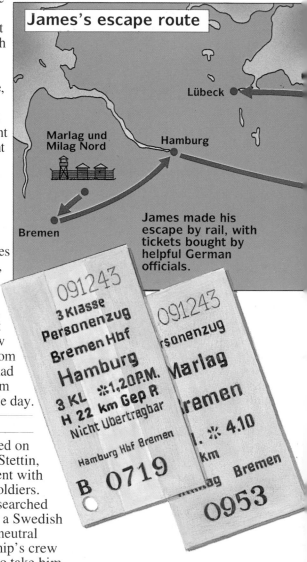

James's escape route

Marlag und Milag Nord

Lübeck

Hamburg

Bremen

James made his escape by rail, with tickets bought by helpful German officials.

091243
3 Klasse
Personenzug
Bremen Hbf
Hamburg
3 KL ✳1.20P.M.
H 22 km Gep R
Nicht übertragbar
Hamburg Hbf Bremen
B 0719

091243
rsonenzug
Marlag
remen
1. ✳ 4.10
km
ag Bremen
0953

He spent a very uncomfortable, uneasy night sleeping at a table opposite a German naval officer and several German sailors. But they must have been even more tired than he was, for they failed to recognize his uniform. Arriving at Lübeck he went first to a barber shop and asked for a shave. Two days of stubble on his chin was beginning to undermine his smart military appearance. This was a near fatal mistake. The

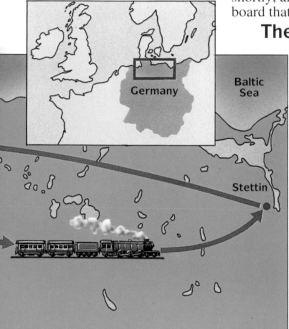

barber looked astonished, and as far as James could understand, said that soap was rationed, and that he had not been offering shaves to his customers for two years. James fled, attracting many a curious glance.

Swedish ships

Feeling flustered, James booked into a hotel, left his suitcase, and headed for the docks. Almost immediately he came upon a couple of Swedish ships. The dock gates were guarded, but James sneaked in by walking behind a goods van that passed between him and the sentry. James walked up the gangplank

of one of the ships, which was loading coal. He knocked on a cabin door and explained who he was, and asked if the crew could take him to Sweden.

The Swedish sailor he spoke to immediately recognized his uniform. He was friendly, but explained that the ship could not take him. They needed to refuel and several German dock hands would be coming aboard. He said that the other Swedish ship was leaving very shortly, and James should board that one.

The tide turns

James begged the Swedish sailor to let him stay. In the three days he had been on the run this was the first time he had felt safe, and now his nerve was going. Even the short walk between these two ships seemed like a huge, unreachable distance. But the Swede was adamant. If James stayed aboard he would be discovered by German dock hands.

As James reluctantly left the ship he saw to his dismay that the one he was heading for was casting off its ropes and leaving the quayside. He debated whether or not to run for the boat and jump onto the deck, but he knew someone would spot him and the boat would be stopped before it left German waters.

Dockyard detention

His luck had run out, and now things really started to go wrong. James was spotted leaving the docks and a guard insisted on taking him to the police station to have his papers thoroughly checked.

At the station a policeman examined the Bulgarian pass with a magnifying glass. The man looked up at him and said "Where did you escape from?". James had been caught.

Cordial captors

The conversation that followed was surprisingly cordial. While one policeman mocked his forged pass, another congratulated James on doing so well with the very limited resources available in a prison camp. He even told James he should have put *Polizei Präsident* instead of *Polizei Kommissar* on one document.

By now James had a small audience, and the local police were quite amused by his tale. The man who escorted him back to the local military jail said he was sorry he had had such bad luck.

Second time lucky

James was sent back to Marlag und Milag Nord, and spent ten days in a punishment cell. But this did not deter him. He escaped five weeks later, this time disguised as a merchant seaman. Taking the same route, he successfully boarded a ship to Sweden. Once in this neutral country he was able to return safely to England.

Knitting needle escape for Soviet master spy

Soviet spy George Blake's escape from prison on October 22, 1966, began with a discussion about wrestling on television. Blake, an inmate of Wormwood Scrubs in West London, asked a guard whether he thought the fights were faked. The guard suspected nothing of the well-behaved prisoner, who was now four years into a 42 year sentence.

But this was no idle chat. The guard became so absorbed in the conversation that he failed to notice another inmate, who was a friend of Blake's, remove two panes of glass from a window above his head.

Outside assistance

Outside the prison, in an alley that separated it from Hammersmith Hospital, another friend of Blake's, Sean Bourke, waited nervously in a car. He carried a large pot of yellow chrysanthemums, and every so often he spoke into them. They concealed a walkie-talkie radio. Blake too had one of these radios, smuggled in by Bourke on a recent visit.

Celebration meal

Bourke had made friends with Blake in prison, and had recently been released. He had been planning this escape for a year and had confidently prepared a meal of steak, and strawberries and cream, to celebrate Blake's release.

When Bourke first arrived at the alley a prison official had frightened him off. But now he was back and waiting impatiently for Blake to let him know when to throw a ladder over the prison wall.

Soviet spy George Blake

Wormwood Scrubs was a huge, drafty, understaffed, Victorian building. Many of its prisoners were small-time criminals, serving short sentences. Blake was an obvious exception, and his removal to a more high-security prison had been requested four times since he arrived there.

Unfortunately there were no suitable prisons for him in London. But the British secret service needed to interview him from time to time, and it was convenient for them to have him in the capital.

Popular prisoner

Despite public outrage caused by his spying, Blake was a popular man in Wormwood Scrubs. He taught illiterate prisoners to read and write and many inmates felt some sympathy for him. A few shared his communist beliefs, while others felt his 42 year sentence was too harsh. He had made several good friends in prison, and now they were prepared to help him escape.

George Blake's patchwork past

Blake came from a mixed background, and his loyalty lay with his belief in communism, rather than with any one country.

He was born in Holland, his mother was Dutch and his father was Egyptian. He fled to Britain during the Second World War, after fighting against the Nazis with the Dutch Resistance.

He became a British citizen and joined the navy, and then MI6, the British secret service.

It was here that he began to work for the communist Soviet Union (now Russia), passing on information about British spies working there and in eastern Europe.

Blake's spying caused outrage in Britain when newspapers reported he had betrayed 40 British spies.

DAILY EXPRESS

No. 18,992   TUESDAY JUNE 20 1961   3 a.m. forecast Sunny   Price 3d

40 AGENTS BETRAYED

AND ALL BY THIS MAN ➤

New shock over spy Blake

By CHAPMAN PINCHER

Torchlight police hunt for nature boy Tony

TREATING THIS AS

2 am: Miners in 'grave danger'

Escape recipe

Sean Bourke

Bourke was Blake's most important ally, and had planned this escape well. He began by contacting Blake's family to raise funds for the scheme. Blake's sister even flew in from Bangkok, where she now lived, to discuss this.

The cost of the escape, Bourke calculated, would be around £700. He worked out exactly what was required to get Blake out of the country, and needed funds to cover the following items:

• One home-made rope ladder to throw over the prison wall – three clothes lines and 30 size 13 knitting needles to make rungs for the ladder.

• Two walkie-talkie radios to communicate between the prison and outside world.

• One pot of chysanthemums to hide the walkie-talkie.

• One set of civilian clothes. (Blake wore a prison uniform.)

• One getaway car – a Humber Hawk.

• One hideaway. (This would need a month's rent paid in advance, plus weekly rent until it was no longer needed.)

• Two boat/plane tickets to Europe.

• Two false passports.

Bourke soon squabbled with the family however, as they wanted him to account for every penny he spent. They were naturally suspicious of a man who had been to prison, and could not be sure that he was a genuine friend of Blake's. They also felt that his plan was too simple to work.

Damning evidence

Bourke, on the other hand, felt it was unreasonable of them to expect him to keep receipts for forged documents, and did not want to store up evidence against himself if the police became suspicious. He turned instead to friends who were sympathetic to Blake, and they provided the money he needed.

BRITISH PASSPORT

UNITED KINGDOM OF GREAT BRITAIN AND NORTHERN IRELAND

202145

Faking a passport

This is how Sean Bourke prepared a fake passport for himself. Due to changes in British passport design this technique is now no longer possible.

①

Remove photograph from stolen passport by holding over steam, taking care not to damage the stamp on it.

②

Mix up quantity of plaster of Paris. Press part of photo with stamp on down hard in plaster of Paris. Leave to set, then remove photo.

③

Place new passport photo on indent in plaster of Paris. Scribble hard over back with pencil.

④

Stamp will be transferred to new photo.

⑤

Place new photo in position on old passport, taking care to match the transferred stamp with the stamp on the passport.

D Hall

Bourke waits in alley.

Blake escapes through window.

Wormwood Scrubs prison in West London. When Blake leapt from the top of the wall into this alley, he broke his wrist.

Escape route blocked

By the autumn of 1966 the escape plan was finalized, but this was nearly ruined by another breakout, which took place in D Hall where Blake himself was held.

Four men broke out of a large window at the end of the hall, which Blake intended to use, and climbed over the prison wall. Plans were immediately made to place wire mesh over all large windows in the prison.

Blake breaks out

The window at D Hall was only a week away from being strengthened when George Blake made his escape. He and Bourke had planned it for a Saturday, between six and seven o'clock. At this time the hall was quiet, with few guards in attendance. Most guards and prisoners were at a weekly film show in the prison theatre.

As soon as Blake was alone he contacted Bourke on his walkie-talkie to make sure he was ready, and headed for the window where a hole had just been made for him. He squeezed through, leapt down to a porch roof, and onto a flat waste container.

From here, he leapt to the ground and his next hurdle was the outer prison wall. This was where Bourke would prove most useful. Using his walkie-talkie, Blake told him he had escaped out of the window and was now by the wall. Bourke was busy trying to get rid of a car containing a courting couple, and did not reply for several minutes.

Blake crouched in the dark expecting to be spotted at any second by a patrolling guard. Eventually Bourke hurled the rope ladder over the 6m (20ft) wall, and Blake climbed up it.

A painful fall

The wait for Bourke had unnerved Blake. He knew that if he was caught he would probably never have another chance. In his desperation to escape he jumped down from the top of the high wall and landed badly, breaking his wrist and cutting his face.

Bundled away

Bourke bundled him into the back of his car, leaving the ladder and chrysanthemums behind. In their haste to get away they nearly ran over two hospital visitors, and bumped into the back of another car. Flustered and near panic, Bourke drove off to merge into the early evening London traffic. He had succeeded in freeing Blake, now he had to keep him hidden.

Bourke had prepared a house near the prison as a hideaway for them both. They would lie low for a month or so, and then try to leave the country. When they arrived there Blake's face was streaming with blood and his left hand hung limp on his wrist. A doctor was clearly going to be needed.

Bourke went off to dump the car, which he was sure the police would soon be looking for. He returned to the house with whiskey and brandy to celebrate their success.

They spent the evening watching television, where news of the escape was interrupting the evening schedule. The next day a sympathetic doctor was found. He fixed Blake's broken wrist, but it was a terribly painful business.

Chrysanthemum calling card

For the next few days the newspapers continued to be full of stories about the escape, many of them quite fantastic. Some newspapers assumed the pot of chrysanthemums Bourke had left at the scene of the escape was a mysterious calling card.

One national radio station even reported a theory that Blake had never been in prison at all. A substitute had been sent in his place and allowed to escape, while Blake had returned to Moscow as a double-agent.

With so much interest in Blake's escape, his liberators began to worry about keeping his location secret. He and Bourke were taken to another house, but had to move shortly after. (The wife of the couple who were sheltering them had told her psychiatrist that they were hiding two men from the police.)

By now Bourke's getaway car, which he had carelessly used his own name to buy, had been found. The police were making intense efforts to locate him, and his name was given to radio, television and newspapers.

Berlin getaway

By early November, the two men were hiding in the home of Bourke's friend Pat Pottle, who had provided some of the funds to finance the escape. Blake was exhausted by his ordeal and anxious to leave the country as soon as possible. It was decided that the safest course of action would be to hide him in a car and drive to communist East Germany*.

Camper van hideaway

Bourke offered to drive, but this idea was quickly rejected. If he was recognized he would be arrested and his car would be searched at once. So another friend, Michael Randle, volunteered. He would take his family and pretend to be going on holiday to East Germany. Money left in the escape fund was used to buy a camper van, and its blanket compartment was enlarged so that Blake could be concealed within it.

Carsick spy

Randle set off on Saturday December 17, reaching East Germany without a hitch. A stiff and slightly carsick Blake was dropped off a short distance outside East Berlin and left to make contact with the local authorities. The East German soldiers he introduced himself to did not believe who he was.

Blake had to argue forcibly to persuade them to contact the Soviet intelligence service in East Berlin. When this was finally done an officer who knew Blake was sent to identify him.

When this man walked in and hugged Blake, shouting "It's him! It's him!", the renegade spy knew his troubles were over. Several days later he was flown to Moscow, the capital of the Soviet Union.

Bourke escapes

Bourke slipped out of the country on a false passport, flying from London to Berlin, and from there to Moscow. He intended to stay in Moscow for a while and then return to his native Ireland when the fuss had died down. The KGB (Soviet secret police) had different ideas.

Michael Randle's Volkswagen camper van. Blake spent most of the 36 hour journey hiding in the blanket box.

They wanted him to stay in the Soviet Union for at least five years more.

Moscow betrayal

Blake and Bourke were naturally delighted to see each other, and several celebration meals followed. They got on so well that Blake suggested that he and Bourke live together. But the two soon quarrelled. Blake had been cordial and charming in Wormwood Scrubs, but now he was arrogant and ill-mannered. He turned on the man who had set him free, and even hinted to the KGB that Bourke should be eliminated. Bourke spent two years trying to persuade the KGB to let him return to Ireland.

Betrayed by his friend and uncomfortable in the Soviet Union, this was a poor reward for someone who had risked everything to assist Blake in his escape. He was finally allowed to go home to Ireland in October, 1968.

Randle drove Blake to communist East Berlin. From there he was flown to Moscow.

Moscow

United Kingdom

Berlin

London

* At the time, the eastern part of Germany was controlled by the Soviet Union.

Plüschow's dockland disguise

For Kapitänleutnant Gunter Plüschow of the German Naval Air Service, the summer of 1915 was the most tedious he had spent in his life. Held captive at Donington Hall prisoner of war camp, England, he was aching to escape and return to fight for his country in the First World War.

The camp itself was not too unpleasant. He received parcels and letters from home, and poured his frustrations into playing endless games of hockey. But Plüschow, a lively, energetic man, found the constraints of captivity difficult to bear.

Chinese dragon

He began the war in one of its more remote battlefields – China. Here he had acquired a Chinese dragon tattoo, an unusual adornment for an officer. The war here had gone badly for Germany, and Plüschow had just managed to escape with his life from a besieged city. He succeeded in boarding a steamship to San Francisco, USA, and made his way to New York, where he took a boat to Italy. (At this stage of the war the USA and Italy were both neutral countries.)

Unfortunately for him, the boat stopped at the British port of Gibraltar where he was arrested as a prisoner of war, and sent on to Donington Hall stately home, near Derby in England.

Oberleutnant Trefftz

At Donington he met with Oberleutnant Trefftz, who spoke English, and knew England well. Plüschow decided they would make a good team, and suggested they escape together. Trefftz agreed, and the two set about plotting their getaway.

Kapitänleutnant Gunter Plüschow of the German Naval Air Service.

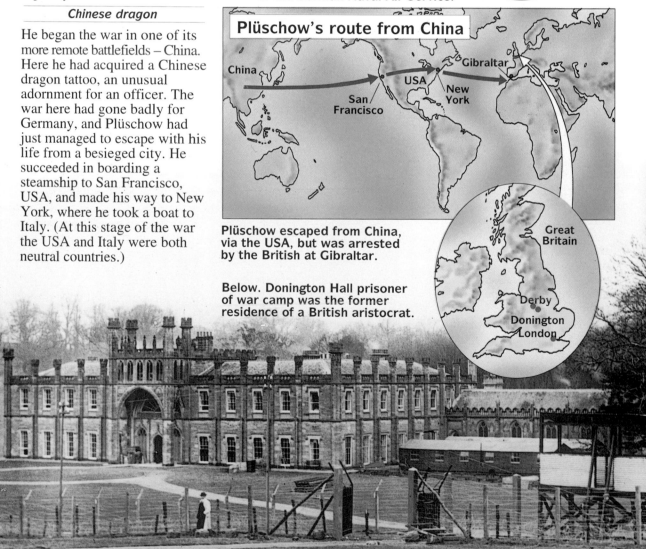

Plüschow's route from China

China · San Francisco · USA · New York · Gibraltar · Great Britain · Derby · Donington · London

Plüschow escaped from China, via the USA, but was arrested by the British at Gibraltar.

Below. Donington Hall prisoner of war camp was the former residence of a British aristocrat.

Plüschow's plan

Plüschow knew from camp gossip that the town of Derby, with its rail link to London, lay a few miles to the north. Once in London he and Trefftz could stow away on a boat heading for a neutral country, such as Holland, and then return to their homeland.

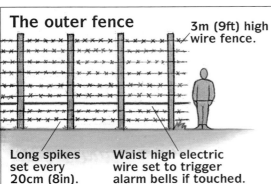

The outer fence

3m (9ft) high wire fence.

Side view of fence

Long spikes set every 20cm (8in).

Waist high electric wire set to trigger alarm bells if touched.

1m (3ft) high coil of barbed wire.

They began by making a detailed study of the guards' routine and camp security. There were two main areas, a day and a night boundary. The day boundary took in the grounds of Donington Hall, which were encircled by a large barbed wire fence. At night, all prisoners retired to the night boundary, which surrounded the camp huts.

Hostile territory

Both men knew breaking out of the camp would be relatively easy. The real difficulty would be crossing hundreds of miles of hostile territory.

Plüschow and Trefftz told their fellow officers about their plans, and enlisted their help to keep their getaway hidden from the camp guards.

Sick list

The escape began on July 4, 1915, when both men claimed to be ill. Their names were placed on the camp sick list, and they were given permission to stay in bed while the other prisoners attended roll call.

After a day of rest, they got up around 4:00pm. Plüschow put on a suit he had bought with him from China, a blue sweater, and a smart grey overcoat. The prisoners wore their own military uniforms around the camp so both men wore officers' caps and coats over their escape outfits.

After they had dressed they ate as many buttered rolls as they could bear, for they knew they were unlikely to find food on their journey.

Garden hiding place

Outside, it was perfect escape weather. Torrential rain fell in sheets. The camp guards stood frozen and miserable in their sentry boxes, in no mood to keep a sharp eye out for escapers.

The two men wandered into the park within the day boundary of the camp. A few footsteps away from the barbed wire perimeter there was a large pile of garden chairs. They looked around to make sure no one was watching them, and then crouched down and hid among the chairs.

An hour passed. The camp clock struck six – the cue for the evening roll call. This was the time when help from their fellow prisoners would be most useful. The two escapers were reported sick, and as soon as the roll call was over, two German officers ran back to Plüschow and Trefftz's beds. The camp guard sent to check on them saw two sleeping figures, and marked them present.

After the roll call the day boundary became forbidden territory for the prisoners, and the sentries withdrew to the night boundary. This left the two escapers outside the guarded area of the camp.

Final hurdle

There was one final hurdle to overcome. Just before bedtime a guard checked on all prisoners by going from hut to hut. Plüschow and Trefftz's comrades knew this routine well. They made sure the two escapers' beds were occupied when the guard entered their rooms.

Footsteps from freedom

Crouching in the dark, the two men listened for any sign that their escape had been discovered. An hour passed. Silently they crept from their hiding place and began an uncomfortable climb over the three barbed wire fences that made up the outer perimeter. They crossed without serious mishap, although Plüschow did tear a large hole in his trousers.

London bound

Once beyond the wire the men discarded their army clothing. As they walked briskly away an English soldier loomed out of the dark. They had already agreed what to do if this occurred. As the man approached the escapers embraced like two lovers and the soldier walked away, tutting with embarrassment.

Shortly afterwards they came to a sign post. It was so dark Trefftz had to climb up it to feel the letters with his fingers. It said "Derby" – they were on the right track.

Roadside wash and brush-up

They walked throughout the night, arriving at the outskirts of Derby as dawn broke. Here they stopped to tidy themselves up. Plüschow repaired his trousers with the needle and thread he always carried with him, and both men shaved, using spit as shaving soap. They headed for the railway station and then separated, agreeing to meet on the steps of St. Paul's Cathedral in London, at seven that evening.

Plüschow's journey passed without incident but that night Trefftz did not appear at St. Paul's. A weary Plüschow made his way to Hyde Park in central London intending to find a quiet place to sleep.

Hedge seat for a concert

The park was closed so he crept into the garden of a nearby house and hid under a thick hedge. After an hour several people came out to enjoy the cool night air. Plüschow, fearing he would be discovered at any moment, lay rigid with fright. As they wandered around, a beautiful soprano voice accompanied by a piano floated out across the garden.

Lulled by the singing, Plüschow drifted off to sleep.

The sound of a policeman's boots tramping along the road woke him early next morning. Fearing he would be spotted, he made his way to Hyde Park, which opened at dawn, and slept on a bench until 9:00am.

Wanted!

His sleep refreshed him, but his spirits sank when he went into a station. A huge poster announced news of his escape. It stated that Trefftz had been captured, and the police were looking for Plüschow.

A newspaper he bought gave a very accurate description of his appearance and tattoo. It went on to say:

"He is particularly smart and dapper in appearance, has very good teeth, which he shows somewhat prominently when talking or smiling, is very English in manner and knows this country well."

Knowing he might be recognized at any time made Plüschow very nervous. He needed to change his appearance at once, starting with his stylish overcoat.

This he decided to leave in a cloakroom at Blackfriars Station. When handing it over, the attendant asked his name. Plüschow's anxiety boiled over. He replied in German:

"Meinen?" (Mine?)

"Oh I see" said the attendant.

"Mr. Mine. M.i.n.e." and handed over a receipt.

Two policemen stood nearby watching inquisitively, no doubt wondering why Plüschow looked so terrified. He needed a quiet spot to hide away and calm down.

On the run in London

Tilbury Docks

London

River Thames

Plüschow arrived in London to find his escape and description featured prominently in the papers. He headed for Tilbury Docks, where he hoped to stow away aboard a boat to Europe.

Blackfriars Station

Hyde Park

River Thames

Blackfriars Station connected London with the coast.

Hyde Park, where Plüschow spent his first night in London.

Hat, collar and tie were thrown into the River Thames. He rubbed Vaseline, boot polish and coal dust into his scalp, to make his blond hair black and greasy. He dirtied his clothes, and found a flat cap to wear.

Dockworker disguise

Smart and dapper Gunter Plüschow was gone. In his place stood George Mine, dock worker. Plüschow even altered his posture, slouching about with hands in pockets, and spitting casually, as he imagined dock workers did.

Next day, on top of a bus he overheard two businessmen talking. They said a Dutch steamer arrived at Tilbury Docks every afternoon, leaving early next morning for Holland. Plüschow caught a train to Tilbury at once.

The Mecklenburg

Arriving at the docks an hour later he went down to the riverside and sure enough, a Dutch steamer, the *Mecklenburg*, arrived. Plüschow decided he would swim out to her under cover of darkness, hide on board, and then jump ship at Holland. But getting aboard was to be more difficult than he imagined.

Stinking, slimy mud

Standing on the river bank Plüschow sank to his hips in stinking, slimy mud. Making a desperate grab for a plank, he saved himself from a horrible drowning death.

The next night he stole a small dinghy, and began to row towards the *Mecklenburg*. But the boat filled with water and ran aground. Plüschow waded wearily through the mud back to dry land.

Finally he succeeded in reaching the steamer with another stolen boat. Climbing the ship's anchor cable and hauling himself on board, he hid under the canvas cover of a lifeboat. In this safe haven he collapsed, and sank into an exhausted sleep.

Across the channel

Plüschow was awakened by the ship's shrill siren several hours later, and peeped from under the canvas cover to see that the *Mecklenburg* was docking in Holland. He was now in a neutral country, and free to travel home. Pulling out his knife, he sliced open the canvas and with a dramatic flourish stood up, revealing himself to all. He expected to be arrested at once by the ship's crew, but much to his surprise, he was ignored completely. The crew were too busy landing the boat, the passengers were preoccupied with their luggage.

Exit forbidden

Ambling off the boat with the passengers, Plüschow sneaked through a door marked "Exit forbidden". He was eager to avoid having to explain himself to customs officials, and once through, he was free.

That night he booked into a hotel, had a long bath, and ate enough for three. The following day, July 13, 1915, he took the train for Germany. Pacing about his compartment, too excited to sit down, he was at last heading for home.

Plüschow as George Mine. Boot polish and Vaseline transformed the dapper German officer.

Tilbury Docks was London's main port for neutral Holland.

Tilbury Docks

Harry Houdini – escaping for a living

The packed theatre crowd simmered with excitement. Harry Houdini had just performed a series of escapes that had left them perplexed and astonished.

He had wrestled out of a straitjacket, and then changed places, in the blink of an eye, with an assistant locked within a rope-bound box. Now he was to perform an escape so dangerous he could drown attempting it.

Underwater terror

An iron can, large enough to hold a man, was placed in the middle of the stage and filled with water. Houdini appeared in a bathing suit and announced he was to be placed inside, and padlocked in.

He told the crowd he would demonstrate how long he could remain underwater, and invited the healthiest among them to hold their own breath as he submerged. Then he stepped into the can and vanished. After one or two minutes the audience were gasping for breath, but Houdini himself emerged three minutes later.

Locked in

Houdini was then handcuffed and taking a final deep breath, he disappeared under the water. A lid was placed on top and secured with locks. A small curtain was placed just in front of the can. A single spotlight shone on the curtain as the theatre band played a tune called *Many Brave Hearts Lie Asleep in the Deep.*

Two minutes went by, then three. The crowd grew anxious. Three and a half minutes passed. Then, a dripping wet Houdini emerged from behind the curtain, breathless but triumphant. The theatre erupted into thunderous applause.

Poster and publicity photograph for the water can trick. Houdini often escaped wearing a swimsuit, to prove to his audience there were no tools or keys hidden in his clothing.

One row of rivets on the can was false. Once the stage curtain was drawn, Houdini pushed up the top of the churn and escaped.

World famous

When Houdini took this act around North America and Europe in 1908, he was the world's most famous escape artist. Many of his audience thought he had magical powers. They said he could vanish into thin air, or slip through a keyhole.

Unique ability

Many of Houdini's tricks relied on deceptions and illusions familiar to most magicians, but he also had two exceptional abilities which made his act unique.

The first sprang from a fascination with locks. There was not a lock in the world he could not pick. He worked this skill into his act by escaping from handcuffs and padlocked manacles. He invited audiences to bring their own locks or cuffs, to prove that the ones he opened up were not fake.

Houdini's other great asset was his body. He was very muscular, fit and agile. His fingers were strong enough to

untie knots or buckles through a canvas bag or straitjacket. His feet were almost as nimble as his hands, and he could also unfasten knots and buckles with his teeth. He trained himself to hold his breath (to allow him to stay underwater) for over four minutes.

New tricks

When he first became famous his act was based mainly around his lock picking abilities. But he realized this would not interest people forever. Part of Houdini's success lay in knowing when to move on. He was constantly striving to offer his audience a new and exciting escape.

Upside-down straitjacket

Escaping from a straitjacket had long been part of his act. It was not a trick – Houdini relied on his own brute strength and agility to wrestle out of this canvas and leather restraint. He kept audiences interested in the stunt by performing it in public, suspended upside down from a construction crane, or dangling from the top of a tall building.

Even more exhausting was the wet sheet escape. Here Houdini was wrapped in two linen sheets, and tied with bandages to a metal frame bed. The sheets were then soaked in warm water, which tightened them around his body. With intense effort, Houdini then proceeded to wriggle out. The trick held a curious fascination for him, and he continued to perform it even though most audiences found it unexciting.

Lock picking

Locks can be opened with a special metal strip or wire (called a pick) instead of a key. A key works in a lock by lifting a series of levers and a skilled lock picker can lift these levers with a pick. This is very difficult and requires a detailed knowledge of the structure of the lock being picked.

Straitjacket escape, Broadway, New York, USA. Stunts such as this generated excellent free publicity for Houdini's stage performances.

Any escape stunt that was suggested by his audience always attracted far more interest than one Houdini concocted himself. He began to accept challenges to escape from boxes or cases that anyone, whether manufacturers or members of the public, could provide. These would be displayed in a theatre foyer, and could be examined by whoever wanted to see them.

A trusted assistant would break into the theatre at night and alter these containers. He would replace long nails with short ones, or file through screws or bolts. He was careful to make sure his tamperings were not discovered, and there was nothing to arouse the suspicions of the audience who watched Houdini emerge, as if by magic, from these containers.

Chinese torture

Another trick, called the Chinese water torture cell, was similar to the water churn escape. Houdini had his ankles placed into wooden stocks and was lowered headfirst into a tank full of water (see poster below). This escape was very popular. Even today, only a handful of people know how he did it.

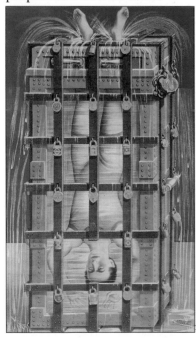

Bridge jumps

Houdini was also an expert at generating his own publicity. He would publicize theatre appearances by leaping off bridges into rivers, tied by chains, or weighed down with an iron ball.

A chained Houdini about to jump into the Charles River, Boston, USA. His wife Bess stands behind him.

One bridge jump in Pittsburg attracted an audience of over 40,000 people. The danger was all too obvious. In the dark water no stage hand could save him if anything went wrong.

When stunts such as this became too familiar to attract much attention, he made them even more daring. In New York in the summer of 1912, a manacled Houdini was nailed into a weighted box, which was then bound with rope and steel cables, and lowered into the East River. As thousands watched, he cheated death before their eyes, emerging from the water moments later.

Near fatal mistakes

The need for constant variety had a price. In a variation of the water can escape, the container was filled with beer.

Houdini was overcome with alcohol fumes, and had to be rescued. On another occasion he was chained up inside the body of a giant squid. Fumes from the chemicals used to preserve the animal nearly killed him. But Houdini was not deterred. Even in his late 40s he continued to think up more daring escapes and stunts. He even planned on escaping from a block of ice, or being buried alive, but both of these were too dangerous to perform.

Houdini and water

Crowds became more excited the longer Houdini stayed underwater, so he trained himself to submerge for as long as possible in his bathtub at home. Iceblocks were also placed in the tub, to get his body prepared for winter bridge jumps.

An untimely death

After a lifetime of genuine danger, his death was the result of an unfortunate incident. In Montreal, a student named J. Gordon Whitehead asked if it was true he could be punched in the stomach without feeling pain. This was so, said Houdini, but first he had to brace himself – that is, tense his muscles. On hearing this Whitehead attacked in a frenzy, lashing out before he was ready.

12 hours to live

Houdini insisted he had not been badly hurt, but he collapsed in Detroit a few days later and was rushed to hospital with a ruptured appendix. Doctors gave him 12 hours to live, but Houdini refused to die. Fighting for his life he told visitors he would soon be back on his feet. But his body was fatally poisoned. He struggled for seven days and died on Halloween – October 31, 1926.

Harry Houdini – A lifetime escaping

1874 Erich Weiss, known as Houdini, is born on March 3, in Budapest, Hungary to Rabbi Samuel and Cecilia Weiss. He is one of six children.

1878 The family move to USA.

1888 Takes job as tie-cutter in New York factory.

1891 Becomes professional magician and escaper. Takes stage name Houdini, after his hero, French magician Robert-Houdon. Spends seven years performing to indifferent audiences, earning $25 a week.

1894 Meets fellow performer Bess Rahmer – one of The Floral Sisters (billed as "Neat Song and Dance Artists"). They marry within a fortnight. Bess becomes his stage assistant. (Houdini is a devoted husband, and writes daily love letters, even though he and his wife are hardly ever apart.)

1899 Hits on the idea of a public "Challenge", where audience is invited to provide their own locks and chains. His wages pick up.

Success in Europe

1900 Travels to Europe. Agent arranges visit to London Police Headquarters. Houdini handcuffed to a pillar by police who say they will return in an hour to free him. Houdini escapes before they have even left the room.

1901 Great success in Germany. Krupps steelworks in Essen make manacles especially for him. Riot at the theatre when thousands turn up to watch him escape.

German police, worried that he is encouraging criminals, accuse him of cheating. Houdini sues. He escapes from locks and cuffs in front of a judge and jury and wins the case.

Challenge to the World

1903 Issues "Challenge to the World". Offers $1,000 to anyone who can better him.

His act is the most popular in Europe. He now earns up to $2,000 a week.

1905 Returns to America where he is equally acclaimed. In one successful publicity stunt he escapes from the

Houdini's films featured dramatic stunts and escapes.

former prison cell of Charles J. Guiteau (assassin of President Garfield in 1881). Further escapes from giant footballs, iron boilers and sealed glass boxes ensure packed out performances.

1906 Begins to publicize shows by jumping off bridges, tied by locks and chains.

1910 Buys aircraft, a Voisin bi-plane, and becomes obsessed with flying. During a trip to Australia, becomes the first person to fly there. Flying takes up so much of his time and energy, his performances suffer, so he gives it up.

1913 Becomes interested in spiritualism (communicating with the souls of the dead) following the death of his mother whom he loved intensely. Although he longs to believe in it, his experience as a magician convinces him that the spirit appearances and voices he witnesses at spiritualist gatherings are fake.

Returns to magic

1918 Tired of escaping, Houdini returns to magic. Despite a show which features a disappearing elephant, audiences are disappointed.

1920 Houdini's interest in spiritualism leads to a friendship with Sir Arthur Conan Doyle – creator of Sherlock Holmes, and a leading spiritualist.

Film failure

1921 Sets up film company to make films featuring escapes. Houdini is a poor actor, and finds love scenes deeply embarrasing. After initial success, company goes bankrupt.

1924 Publishes a book, *A Magician Among the Spirits,* which describes spiritualism as a fraud. Doyle is deeply offended, and his friendship with Houdini ends.

1926 Following a violent assault in Montreal, Houdini collapses in Detroit. He dies of a burst appendix, on October 31, and is buried next to his mother in New York.

Colditz Castle – escape-proof ?

Towering over the town of Colditz, in east Germany, is a grey granite, high-walled castle. During the Second World War it was used as a high-security prison for persistent escapers from German prisoner of war camps. Nazi Reichsmarschall Hermann Goering visited and declared it escape-proof.

International escapers

The castle could hold 800 prisoners – men from all over the world who had fought against Nazi Germany. There were over 800 guards. Every day of the year, four times a day, a parade was held where every man was counted. Sometimes the men were even called out in the dead of night, and stood shivering for hours, until their captors were satisfied that every one of the prisoners was present.

Soldiers with guard dogs stalked the courtyards and catwalks which covered the high walls and battlements. Machine gun posts were set up on roofs and watchtowers. At night searchlights probed every shadow. Sound detectors listened for digging noises, or any other clues of escapers at work.

Over, under, or disguise

Despite these fierce restrictions hundreds of escape attempts were made between 1939 and 1945. As with any prison there were basically two ways out. One was to perfect a convincing disguise and walk out of the castle gates under the noses of the guards. This required great courage, but worked for some. The other was to find a way over or under the castle walls with the minimum risk of death or detection.

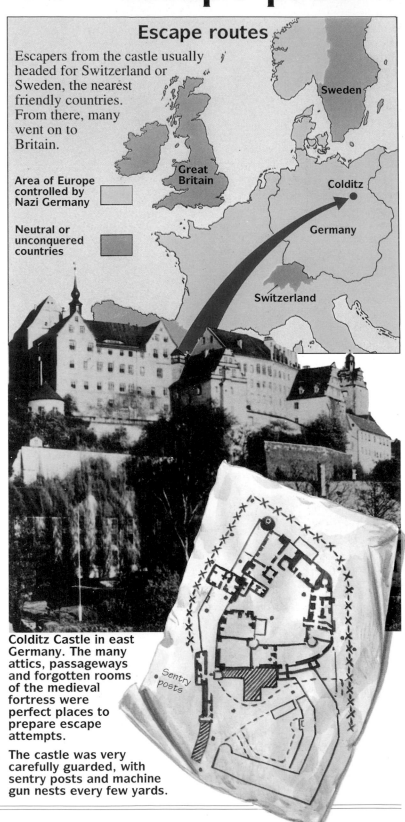

Escape routes

Escapers from the castle usually headed for Switzerland or Sweden, the nearest friendly countries. From there, many went on to Britain.

Sweden

Great Britain

Colditz

Germany

Switzerland

Area of Europe controlled by Nazi Germany

Neutral or unconquered countries

Colditz Castle in east Germany. The many attics, passageways and forgotten rooms of the medieval fortress were perfect places to prepare escape attempts.

Sentry posts

The castle was very carefully guarded, with sentry posts and machine gun nests every few yards.

Sheet rope escape

Some escapers tried the most obvious routes out of the castle. In May 1941, two Polish officers, Lieutenants Surmanowicz and Chmiel, made a rope of knotted bed sheets.

Attic breakout

They broke into an attic which had a window overlooking the castle wall, and began to climb carefully down the 37m (120ft) drop. Unfortunately Chmiel's heavy boots made a loud scraping sound as they passed by the guardroom window. The two were spotted at once by a suspicious officer and guns were swiftly pointed at the helpless escapers.

The Polish prisoners' sheet rope. Such obvious escape plans were usually unsuccessful.

Doomed escapes

The authorities at Colditz used several strategies to demoralize escapers. Sometimes, when an escape plan was discovered, the camp guards let the prisoners continue with their efforts. They felt it was better to have inmates working on a project they knew about, than on one they did not.

They also felt that stopping an escape at the last moment, after so much painstaking planning, would be more disheartening, and discourage prisoners from plotting further escapes.

Wasted – eight months of digging for their lives

Most escapes involved months of preparation. In 1941, 21 French officers spent eight months digging a tunnel which began underneath the castle clock tower. The entrance was reached by climbing 33m (110ft) down the inside of the tower on a rope ladder. After several weeks of digging, the guards realized a tunnel was being built. They noticed a ceiling beam in the French quarters had begun to crack. A search of the attic above revealed huge heaps of earth and rock.

Top to bottom search

The tunnel entrance was so cleverly hidden however, that a top to bottom search of the castle failed to find it. In the middle of the night the French could even be heard digging away, but still their tunnel could not be found.

Eventually their luck ran out.

A German officer remembered that the clock tower had only been given the briefest of inspections in the initial search. The floorboards at the top of the tower were removed, and a small guard was lowered into the dark shaft. At once he heard the French digging away. Soldiers were immediately sent to the tower basement where the entrance was discovered. By now the tunnel reached beyond the castle walls and eight months' work had been wasted, only days before an escape could have been made.

The entrance to the tunnel was hidden in a disused wine cellar underneath the castle clock tower.

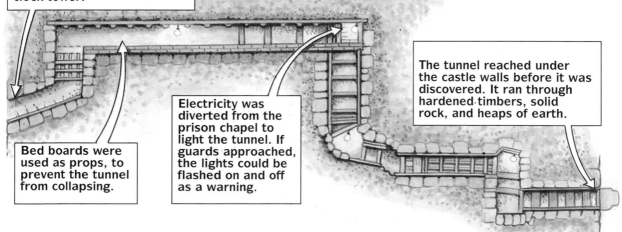

Bed boards were used as props, to prevent the tunnel from collapsing.

Electricity was diverted from the prison chapel to light the tunnel. If guards approached, the lights could be flashed on and off as a warning.

The tunnel reached under the castle walls before it was discovered. It ran through hardened timbers, solid rock, and heaps of earth.

Dummy Moritz dupes guards while two escape down drain

There were other, more cunning attempts to break out of the castle. A group of Dutch prisoners discovered a manhole in a park next to the castle, where men were taken to exercise. It would be a perfect place to leave a couple of escapers behind.

Cloak camouflage

The first to try out the manhole were Lieutenants Larive and Steinmetz. For the plan to work they needed the help of their fellow prisoners. On the day of the escape they were smuggled into the park by a group of Dutch inmates, hidden beneath the cloaks of the two tallest men. The escapers had not been counted by the guards on the way to the park, so they would not be missed on the way back.

Once in the park the group gathered and pretended to hold a Bible class, huddling close around the manhole. Larive and Steinmetz, hidden by the crowd, eased off the cover with a makeshift lever and climbed inside.

Dutch officers with Moritz the dummy.

To conceal their absence at the next parade two dummies, dubbed Max and Moritz, had been created. A Polish officer who was an amateur sculptor, made two heads with plaster. This was obtained by bribing a local builder who frequently visited the castle. Paint stolen from prison art classes added realistic features. The heads were placed on long army coats, and carried like ventriloquist dummies. In the middle of a rank of men they went unnoticed.

An escape success

That night, the two Dutchmen emerged from the manhole to begin a successful escape to Switzerland. Over the next few weeks four more men escaped in this way (although two were later recaptured). The scheme eventually fell apart when guards noticed another two men being smuggled into the manhole. The dummies were not found until several months later, and were used to cover roll call absences for other escapers.

Escape equipment

In order to escape across hostile territory, the right clothes, fake passes, maps, and a compass, were all invaluable. Here are some of the ingenious items manufactured in Colditz to help escapers on their way.

Forged travel document. A typewriter was built to imitate typefaces on official German documents. Each letter was carved from wood.

Fake document stamps cut from linoleum.

Compass in walnut shell.

Playing cards. The backs peeled off. Put together in the right order they would make a map.

Rooftop flight

The most daring escape plan of all involved the use of a glider, which was designed and built by a team of British airmen led by Flight Lieutenants Jack Best and Bill Goldfinch. It had a 10m (33ft) wingspan and was large enough to carry two men.

Secret workshop

The glider was built over ten months at one end of a long attic and hidden from view by a false wall made of wood and hessian fabric. This was camouflaged with plaster and mud to match the shade of the surrounding walls. Jack Best, who had been a farmer in Kenya, had learned how to make African mud huts, so he supervised its construction.

Cigarette bribe

The false wall was discovered by a German guard. Luckily for the British he used this information to bargain with the glider builders, rather than report it to his officers. He agreed to keep quiet about the wall in exchange for 500 cigarettes. This guard later died from natural causes, but a story went around that

The Colditz glider

The glider carried two men. It was covered in cotton fabric and held together with glue.

The frame was made of wood taken from bed boards and the theatre stage.

The nose was made of papier-mâché.

Electrical and telephone wires linked the cockpit controls with the wing and tail ailerons, and the rudder.

his demise was caused by smoking too many cigarettes.

Bathtub launching

The airmen intended to launch the glider by carrying it out to a flat roof next to their attic workshop. They would place it on a trolley, which would be attached to a long rope tied to a bathtub full of concrete.

They calculated that if the tub was pushed off the roof it would fall with sufficient speed to pull the glider fast enough to launch it into the air, when it went off the edge of the roof. The rope would be released and the craft would glide silently onto the meadows outside the castle. Here its crew could make good their escape.

This dangerous plan could easily have resulted in the death of the escapers, and fortunately it was never tried out. By the time the glider was completed, in January 1945, the prisoners knew from their secret radio sets that the war was drawing to an end and would soon be over.

One in ten

During the war there were over 300 escape attempts from Colditz Castle. Most ended in immediate recapture or even death. Despite this, 130 men succeeded in getting away from the "escape-proof" castle. Although many were arrested trying to reach friendly territory, 30 managed to get home safely.

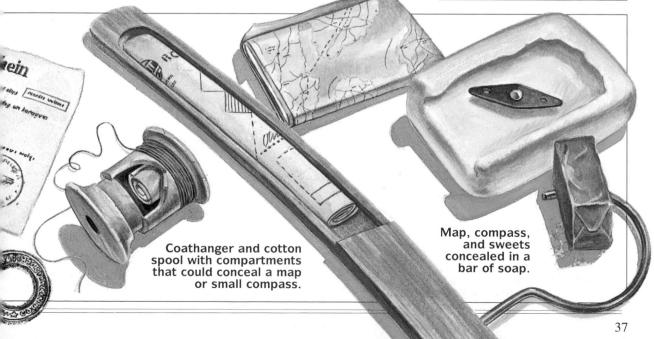

Coathanger and cotton spool with compartments that could conceal a map or small compass.

Map, compass, and sweets concealed in a bar of soap.

Electricians, officers and German housewives

Not every escape attempt from Colditz involved such intense physical effort or danger. It was possible for a prisoner to walk out of the castle right under the gaze of the guards, if he was wearing a convincing enough disguise.

The electrician's double

André Perodeau (left), attempts to impersonate electrician Willy Pöhnert (right).

One French officer, Lieutenant André Perodeau had noticed a close resemblance between himself and the castle electrician, a local tradesman named Willy Pöhnert. Not only did they look alike, but they were almost the same age, height and weight. They even wore similar glasses. Perodeau hoped a good impersonation might enable him to escape.

Perodeau had tried a similar scheme before. He had been sent to Colditz following an escape from his previous prisoner of war camp, where he had disguised himself as a refuse collector. He had got out of the camp, but was recaptured only hours later.

He began to observe Pöhnert closely, and tried to copy his walk and posture. Clothes were found to match the electrician's, and when no suitable match existed, they were made from bed clothes, blankets and sheets, and dyed the correct shade. A forged pass with Pöhnert's name on it was also prepared for him.

The escape was planned for a December evening. An impostor would be harder to spot in the dark. There was a good chance too that the guards may be toasting the coming Christmas with a few drinks, and be less vigilant than usual.

A well-timed arrival

The French sabotaged the electricity in their living quarters, so that Pöhnert would be summoned to the castle. They timed it so the electrician would arrive just before the guard changed. Perodeau did not want to walk past the same sentries who had let Pöhnert in.

After checking that Pöhnert had in fact arrived, Perodeau put on his disguise and walked toward the first of four checkpoints. His pass was glanced at, and the gate was unlocked. As he walked through, the sentry asked him a question. Perodeau spoke almost no German but he was prepared for this, and had practiced his reply. *"Ich habe etwas vergessen."* (I have forgotten something.)

He walked on to the next checkpoint, but this time his pass was examined carefully. It contained a number of glaring mistakes. The guard became suspicious, and kept looking up from the pass and asking questions. Not understanding him Perodeau could only stand and stare. The escape had failed.

A hat and wig

The problem of getting past the prison checkpoints could be avoided by taking on a disguise outside the castle. Frenchman Lieutenant Boulé was one escaper who tried to do this.

He and his fellow officers marched to the local park every day to exercise. Boulé had noticed that at one point on the journey they turned a corner and were briefly out of sight of the guards. This was where he would change his appearance.

So one day he wore women's clothing under his long army coat, and when he turned this particular corner he took off the coat, popped a hat and wig onto his head, and began to walk the other way. This worked perfectly until he dropped his watch. A British soldier, who did not know what Boulé was doing, picked it up and gave it to a guard, pointing at "the lady" who had dropped it. The guard shouted after him, and Boulé, assuming he had been spotted, gave himself up.

Lieutenant Boulé disguised as a German woman.

Failure photographed

The photographs here were taken by the Germans as evidence of unsuccessful escape attempts. The shots were shown to new guards to warn them what to expect from the prisoners.

The Nazi officers

The British and Dutch worked together on the most daring disguise of all – that of a German officer. Uniforms were tailored and dyed to resemble officers' overcoats, and suitable rank badges were carved from wood, and painted gold and silver.

A passageway leading to the German quarters of the castle had been discovered. Two escapers dressed as Germans could make their way down it, and then walk out of the castle. Englishman Airey Neave and Dutchman Toni Luteyn (who spoke perfect German) were chosen to try this out.

A swaggering air

On a freezing January evening, the two men walked out of the German quarters of the castle with a slowness to match the dignity of their rank. They swaggered along as sentries opened gates and doors, snapping to attention as they passed by.

However, on their way out of the castle one soldier began to stare at them suspiciously. Luteyn, feeling that their bluff was about to be called, shouted angrily in German "Why do you not salute?". The soldier promptly complied, and the two impostors walked on.

They scrambled over an oak fence, and then had to climb a high stone wall. By now, both were numb with cold and it was difficult to grip the icy surface of the wall. Luteyn's fingers failed him, and Neave had to haul him over. But the two men were out of Colditz, and three days later they had managed to steal through Germany to the safety of neutral Switzerland.

Making a fake uniform

Neave and Luteyn adapted their own uniforms to look like German uniforms, dyed them to match, and added buttons and insignia made from materials available in the camp.

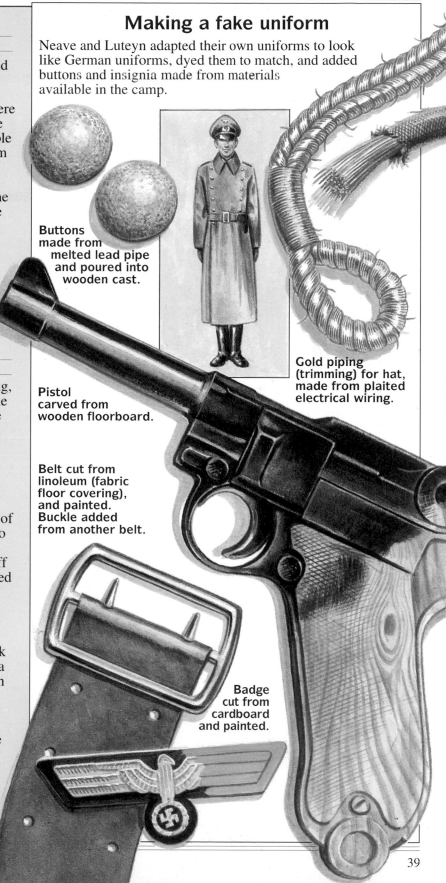

Buttons made from melted lead pipe and poured into wooden cast.

Gold piping (trimming) for hat, made from plaited electrical wiring.

Pistol carved from wooden floorboard.

Belt cut from linoleum (fabric floor covering), and painted. Buckle added from another belt.

Badge cut from cardboard and painted.

Harriet "Moses" Tubman leads slaves to freedom

One August afternoon in 1844, on a farm in Maryland, USA, a black slave named Harriet Tubman was chopping wood under a hot sun. The work was hard, but she dare not stop to rest, for fear of being beaten.

As she worked a shadow fell over her, and she looked up to see a white woman watching her. The woman smiled sympathetically and began to talk in a friendly way. She asked about the welts that covered Tubman's neck, and the huge scar that ran across the top of her head. Tubman explained that the welts were the consequence of several childhood whippings.

When she was seven she had been sent to work in the home of her owner. She had to clean and polish and look after her mistress's children. This was exhausting work for such a young child, but if she ever fell asleep she was callously whipped.

The scar was a more recent injury, caused by a badly aimed iron weight, thrown at another slave by a brutal overseer.

The white woman looked around to make sure that they were alone. She drew closer and quietly explained that she lived on a farm nearby, and that if Tubman was ever in trouble she was prepared to help her.

Harriet Tubman was nicknamed "Moses" after the biblical character who led his tribe from slavery to freedom.

Secret association

This was Harriet Tubman's first contact with "the underground railroad" – a secret organization which helped thousands of black slaves to escape from the farms and plantations of the southern USA.

Slave master dies

Shortly after this meeting, Tubman's slave master died. Although she had no love for him this was a great blow. Tubman lived with her husband and family on his farm, and his death would probably mean that all his slaves would be sold to other farms and plantations. The owners did not care if this meant that families would be broken up.

Naturally Tubman did not want her family to be separated, so she tried to persuade them to all run away together. Her family were too afraid to go, however, as runaway slaves were whipped if they were recaptured. But Tubman had suffered enough. She decided to escape alone.

In this poster of 1853 a trader offers $1,200 or more for negro slaves. Harriet Tubman's rescue missions cost slave owners so much money that they offered $40,000 for her recapture.

This painting by W.A. Walker shows slaves working on a cotton plantation in the south of the USA, before the civil war.

Slavery in the USA

Two hundred years ago slavery was legal in
the USA. Slaves were shipped from Africa to
work in plantations in the southern states. They
produced cotton and tobacco and other goods.

**The whip was
the most common
punishment for
escapers.**

United States

**This whip has a
leather thong
attached to
an iron
chain.**

Slave states
in the USA

States where slavery
was not permitted.

**Pronged neck
ring. A slave
who wore such
a device could
not even lie down
to sleep.**

Slaves were regarded as property, and
could be sold, like a piece of furniture,
or a house. Slaves who ran away and were
recaptured faced cruel punishments, some
of which are shown here. Slavery was abolished
in the USA in 1865 following the American Civil
War between northern and southern states. Around
4 million slaves were freed.

**These hooks were designed
to catch in brambles and
branches and prevent
slaves from escaping.**

**Slave auction in
New Orleans.**

**This headpiece was hung
with bells, which would
make a furtive escape
almost impossible.**

**Most slave houses were simple
wooden shacks, with few comforts.**

**Slaves were sometimes branded
with the initials of their owner,
like farm animals are today.**

Led by a star

Tubman slipped away one day, carrying only a small bag of food. She hurried over to the house of the woman she had met while chopping wood.

The woman recognized her at once and explained three essential rules for escape. She must head for the north of the United States, where slavery was not permitted, she should travel by night, and she should always follow the North Star.

Stations and tickets

Tubman also discovered more about the "underground railroad". This organization used the language of the railroad to describe the work they did. Slaves were "passengers". A friendly house was a "station". A letter telling a fugitive how to find such a house was a "ticket". Anyone accompanying a runaway slave from one station to another was a "conductor".

The woman gave Tubman some money, and a description of a farm house that she was to head for. She told the slave to hurry before her owner sent dogs to trail her scent.

Tubman ran off and eventually found this house. A white woman came to the door and hurried Tubman inside. She gave her new clothes, and burned the old ones, explaining that this would stop the dogs from following her scent.

The night horse and cart

When night fell, a man arrived with a horse and cart. He told Tubman to lie on the floor of the cart and covered her with straw. They drove all night, and the next morning she was told to spend the day hiding in a wood and continue her journey north that evening.

The man gave her a ticket to the next house, and so she continued, for nearly 160km (100 miles).

Free at last

Once out of Maryland she headed through New Jersey to New York, where slavery had been abolished since 1799. Here she found a job in a hotel, working as a cook.

Although she was delighted to be free, Tubman was alone

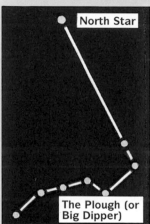

How to find the North Star

North Star

The Plough (or Big Dipper)

The North Star, known to astronomers as Polaris, is directly above the North Pole, so it shows which direction is north. If you live in the northern part of the world you can find it by looking for a group of stars called the Plough (also known as the Big Dipper). A line through the end of the Plough points to the North Star.

in this huge city. She decided to return to Maryland and bring out the rest of her family.

She took a terrible risk returning to the village where she used to live. It was likely that she would be recognized, and there was a reward for her recapture. To hide her identity Tubman disguised herself as an old lady, and wore a big old sun-bonnet to cover the scar on her head. The first couple of trips were successful, and she managed to bring back a sister and a brother. Then she returned for a third time to rescue her husband, John Tubman.

Tubman's heartbreak

But John Tubman had thought his wife was dead, and when she found him he was living with another woman. Although Harriet Tubman was upset, it

did not discourage her. Determined not to waste a journey, she returned to the north with another group of runaway slaves. They were so grateful to be free that Tubman decided to help whoever she could, and not just her own family.

Using the money earned as a cook, Tubman turned herself into a one woman escape organization, returning time and time again to the farms and plantations of the south.

$40,000 reward

But slave owners began to fight back. The underground railroad was becoming too successful. Tubman's fame spread with every rescue, and a $40,000 reward was offered for her capture.

In 1850 the government was persuaded by slave owners to introduce the Fugitive Slave Law. This made the work of the underground railroad much more difficult. Slaves who had escaped to the north could be recaptured, and anyone who helped them escape could be fined or imprisoned.

A hostile stranger

On one expedition soon after this, Tubman went to a house which served as one of the stations on her route. A stranger answered the door and told her angrily that the occupiers had been arrested for helping slaves escape.

Tubman and her group of runaways were in great danger. She knew the stranger would alert the local police and so hid her group on a grassy island on a nearby river. It was midwinter and rain fell unceasingly. The group spent a miserable day shivering in the grass, too frightened to talk to each other.

That evening they saw a man walking along the river bank, dressed as a preacher and carrying a Bible. As he walked he read aloud, as if from the book. Tubman knew the Bible well, but she did not recognize these words. He was saying that there was a wagon in the farmyard across the road, and a horse in the stable. The preacher walked on, calling out his message as he went along.

When it got dark, Tubman and her group went over to the farm. There was a wagon, and a horse, just as the preacher had said. Food and blankets had also been left for the fugitives.

They drove throughout the night to the next station on the route. Here their helpers had not been arrested, and the escape party were able to carry on until they reached Canada. Due to the Fugitive Slave Law this was now the safest place to head for.

Go on or die!

Tubman had one rule for escapers. Once they agreed to go there was no turning back. She carried a pistol, and if anyone dropped down exhausted and refused to go on she would point the gun at their head and say "Dead men tell no tales. Go on or die". She never did shoot anybody, and no one was recaptured and tortured into betraying the secrets of the underground railroad.

Slavery abolished

Between 1860 and 1865 a bitter civil war took place in the United States between the northern and southern states. During the conflict Tubman worked for the North as a scout, spy and nurse.

The war ended with victory for the North. Slavery was abolished and Tubman's work ended. Altogether she had made an extraordinary 19 trips on the underground railroad, and rescued between 300 and 400 slaves.

Midnight welcome at Levi's refuge

Most of the stations on the underground railroad were the houses of freed slaves, but many white Americans also provided shelter. Many were Christians with a deep hatred of slavery, and who suffered fines and imprisonment, and even branding, for their trouble. Despite the threat of such punishments the railroad network carried between 75,000 and 100,000 passengers before slavery was abolished. One famous station was operated by a Quaker named Levi Coffin, who appears in the painting above. He wrote about his experiences in his book *Reminiscences*. Coffin lived at Newport, Wayne County, Indiana, near Cincinnati, where he was a successful businessman.

His wealth and influence in his community protected him from harassment or arrest. His house became a station from the mid 1820s. Three routes, from Cincinnati, Madison and Jeffersonville all converged on his house. When it became known in that area that he helped slaves, he lost many customers, but his business was strong enough to survive. He was prosperous enough to be able to keep a wagon and horses in constant readiness for passengers. Coffin says in his book that rarely a week went by without a knock at the door in the dead of the night.

He was a generous man, and because of his wealth he could afford to look after slaves whose health had suffered during their escape.

His account tells of the condition of his visitors when they arrived. "Sometimes fugitives come to our house in rags, and almost wild, having been out for several months, hiding in thickets during the day, being lost and making little headway at night, particulary in cloudy weather, when the north star could not be seen, sometimes almost perishing for want of food, and afraid of every white person they saw..."

United States of America

Newport

Indiana

Escape or death for Devigny

André Devigny, shackled and alone in Montluc Military Prison in Lyon, was awaiting a death sentence. This French Resistance fighter had been imprisoned here by the Gestapo* in April 1943. He had been brutally beaten, and now he was to face a firing squad.

Montluc Military Prison, in Lyon, France, held captured French Resistance members.

France
Lyon

Impossible escape

Escape seemed almost impossible. He was on an upper floor of the prison, and a solid oak door blocked his way. If he succeeded in breaking through the door he would have to clamber up to a skylight leading to the roof, creep across a courtyard, climb on top of another block, and then sneak over the outer wall of the prison. At any stage, he could be shot on sight. But he was to be executed, so there was nothing to lose.

A pin for a pick

Shortly after Devigny arrived at Montluc, a fellow prisoner offered him a glimmer of hope by giving him a pin to pick the lock on his handcuffs. The cuffs were very basic and could be opened by pushing down a spring inside the lock. He was told how to do this by a prisoner in the next cell who tapped messages to him. (The code was simple – a tap for each letter of the alphabet: A was one tap, followed by a pause, B was two taps, and so on.) It took time, but prisoners have more than enough time on their hands.

His door was also not as formidable as it looked.

A prison spoon was turned into a chisel.

It was made of oak but the beams that held it to its frame were made of softer wood. A sharp tool could lever them off.

Devigny did not have such a sharp tool, but he had been given an iron spoon. He took off his handcuffs when he felt sure he would not be disturbed and scraped the spoon on his cell door making a sharp edge.

He also began to make a rope. Using a razor blade slipped to him by another prisoner, he cut bedding and clothing into thin strips. These he plaited together, strengthening the strands with wire from his mattress. At the end of the rope he attached iron prongs pilfered from a light shade. These would serve as a grappling hook, anchoring the rope to any object it was thrown over.

New arrival

Just before he planned to go, the Gestapo placed another prisoner in his cell, a teenager named Gimenez. This was very awkward. If Devigny escaped and Gimenez did not raise the alarm, he would be shot. Devigny would have to take Gimenez with him.

Shortly before midnight one moonless August evening, Devigny removed a section of the cell door with his sharpened spoon. He and Gimenez squeezed out and headed for the skylight.

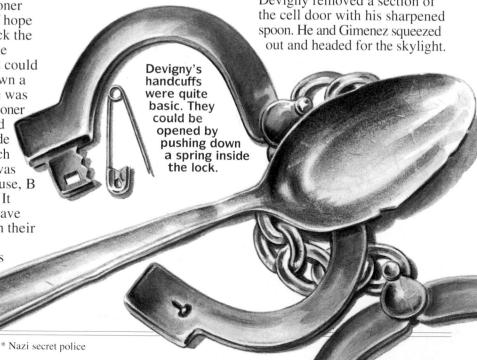

Devigny's handcuffs were quite basic. They could be opened by pushing down a spring inside the lock.

* Nazi secret police

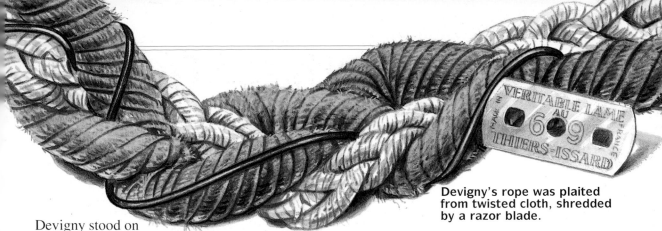

Devigny's rope was plaited from twisted cloth, shredded by a razor blade.

Devigny stood on his cellmate's shoulders. After several attempts he managed to wriggle out. Four months in prison had weakened him, and already he felt exhausted.

Gimenez followed, and the two stood on the roof, panting for breath under a clear night sky. Now they were outside, any sound they made could alert the guards. Fortunately a railway line passed by the prison, so they moved only when a train thundered by.

Cigarettes and bayonets

Trains came every ten minutes and gradually the two crept a little farther along their route to the outer wall. They reached the roof parapet and looked down on the courtyard below. Straining into the gloom, they could pick out the shapes of the guards, where a glowing cigarette end, or a glimmer of light on a bayonet or buckle gave their positions away. Unfortunately, one sentry stood directly in their path.

The prison clock chimed midnight, and signalled the changing of the guard. Devigny watched the new sentry for an hour, studying his routine. As another train passed, he and Gimenez lowered their rope into the dark.

As the clock struck one, Devigny climbed over, not even knowing if the rope was long enough to reach the ground. He slid down so quickly he tore his hands, then ran across the courtyard and hid behind a wall. The sentry stood before him.

A grim choice

Devigny came to a harrowing decision. The only way to get past this sentry was to kill him. As the man turned, Devigny sprang from the shadows, grabbed him by the throat, and strangled him.

When he was dead, Devigny whistled up to Gimenez to join him. Now they had to scale a wall and a roof. Devigny was too weak to climb the wall so Gimenez scrambled up and passed down the rope. From here they climbed over a sloping roof that took them to the edge of the prison. They had a good view of the wire around the prison perimeter. 5m (18ft) separated them from freedom. A single guard cycled by every three minutes.

Despair and relief

A voice drifted up to them. Two other guards must be hidden in the dark. This would make an escape almost impossible. The men were filled with despair, but then realized the voice they heard was the cyclist talking to himself.

They would have to choose their moment carefully, but the urge to hurry was intense. An open cell door and a dead sentry were both waiting to be discovered.

The clock struck three. Devigny waited for the sentry to cycle by, and then threw the rope over the outer wall. The grapple gripped and they pulled the rope tight, and tied it to the roof.

A final risk

The guard came around again, cycling beneath the rope. Dawn was breaking. Time was running out. Both men feared that their rope would snap as they crossed over, leaving them injured in the perimeter, or stranded on the roof. So near to success, neither believed that their luck would hold.

The sky grew lighter still. The circling guard even stopped beneath them to rest for a while, but he never did look up. Eventually, after a fiercely whispered argument about who should go first, Devigny scrambled across, and Gimenez followed.

Early morning shift

Once over the perimeter, the two men crawled along the top of the wall to a section where it was low enough to jump down. Both were dressed in civilian clothes, as the prison had no uniform, and once outside they walked down the street, mingling with a crowd of workmen on their way to start the early morning shift at a local factory. By the time the guards at Montluc had discovered their open cell door and the dead body of the sentry, Devigny and Gimenez had vanished into the countryside.

Breakout at Pretoria Prison

By December 1979 Tim Jenkin, Stephen Lee and Alex Moumbaris were finally ready to tackle the ten locked doors that lay between them and the streets outside Pretoria Prison, South Africa.

Jenkin and Lee, who had been friends since university, had been plotting this escape since their arrival here in June 1978. Neither was prepared to sit out the 12 and eight year sentences imposed on them for being active members of the African National Congress (ANC), a political party that had been banned in South Africa.

Hatching a plot

They soon discovered that most of their fellow prisoners had reconciled themselves to long sentences and abandoned any hope of escape from this top security prison. But not Alex Moumbaris, a fellow ANC member, who had been given

Tim Jenkin (left), Alex Moumbaris (middle) and Stephen Lee (right).

Pretoria top security prison, South Africa. The cells overlooked a courtyard watched over by a fierce dog and armed guards.

a 12 year sentence in 1973. When Jenkin mentioned that they were planning a breakout, Moumbaris replied that if any escape plans were being hatched then "he would definitely like to be one of the chickens".

Political prisoners

Pretoria Prison, built in the 1960s, was an L-shaped, three floor building containing 52 cells. Those convicted of illegal political activity, such as Jenkin, Lee and Moumbaris, were kept separately in one corridor on the first floor. The rest of the cells were occupied by men awaiting trial.

The cell windows overlooked a large yard, containing a garden and tennis court, encircled by a 6m (20ft) high fence. Above the yard was a glass-covered catwalk, which held an armed guard. At night the yard was lit by dazzling searchlights, and occupied by a savage dog, trained to rip any escaper to pieces. It seemed to be formidable, but if Pretoria Prison had any weak spots, then Jenkin, Lee and Moumbaris were determined to exploit them.

Jail routine

Like any prisoners they soon became wearily familiar with the jail's routines. But this could be a tremendous advantage to a would-be escaper. The three were soon able to predict almost exactly what their guards were doing at any time of the day. This enabled them to judge when they were least likely to be disturbed, for example, during the guards' meal times. They also discovered that at night, when everyone was locked in their cell, there was only one warder on duty.

Good manners

Moumbaris was usually hostile and insolent to his jailors, and refused to keep his cell tidy. But Jenkin and Lee realized that aggressive prisoners were watched more closely. They managed to persuade him to be more pleasant to his captors, and as a result he was left alone much more. This intimate knowledge of

Locks, tumblers and counterfeit keys

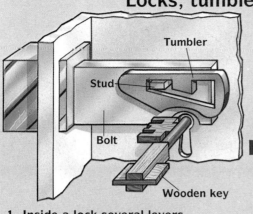

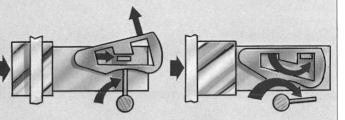

In Pretoria Prison ten locked doors lay between a cell and the streets outside. In order to escape, Jenkin, Lee and Moumbaris had to learn how locks worked, and how to make wooden or metal keys that would open them.

Tumbler

Stud

Bolt

Wooden key

1. Inside a lock several levers, called tumblers, hold a bolt in place against a stud, and prevent it from moving.

2. When a key is turned, it lifts the tumblers over the stud.

3. As the key turns it also draws back the bolt, allowing the door to be opened.

Making a key

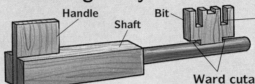

The escapers made separate components for the keys in the prison workshop. They were then put together and filed into shape in the privacy of their cells. Their wooden keys looked like the one shown on the right.

Handle

Shaft

Bit

Cuts. These lift the lock tumblers, and must be shaped to fit a particular lock.

Ward cutaways. These need to match the shape of the lock keyhole, or the key cannot be turned.

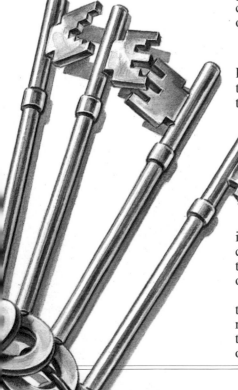

the prison's routine, and a more relaxed relationship with the guards enabled the three to concentrate on their main objective of getting out.

4:30 lockup

Part of the prison routine was that prisoners were locked in their cells at 4:30 each afternoon.

Before then, they were allowed access to certain areas of prison and the exercise yard. This gave them ample opportunity to study escape routes. The simplest route was to break into the yard and attempt to climb over the outer wall, but this also carried the greatest risk of death or serious injury.

Jenkin and Moumbaris began to test out the first hurdle on this route – the yard dog – which they hoped to divert with scraps of food. Several dogs were used on a weekly rota, and although some were prepared to take food off the men, they were highly unpredictable.

After several weeks of deliberating, the three men decided that the safest route out was the way they had come in – through ten locked doors. This would involve making forged keys for each of these doors and developing lock picking skills which none of them possessed. It would take a huge amount of time, but that was one thing they had more than enough of.

Only one chance

They knew there would only be one chance to escape. If they were caught in their attempt, they would be marked down as troublesome prisoners. Several years could be added to their sentences. Supervision would be considerably tighter, and they could even be sent to a much tougher prison.

Jangling taunts

The keys for the locks they needed were all around them. The guards carried them on their waists, in big jangling bunches. Jenkin thought they enjoyed waving them around, demonstrating the power they had over their prisoners. But, extraordinarily enough, there were some keys that were left in locks, in areas that prisoners had access to during the day.

Stealing these would be too obvious. It would alert the guards to a possible escape, and the cells would all be searched from top to bottom in the hunt for the missing keys. Any key they needed would have to be copied.

Material and tools to do this could be stolen from the prison workshop, where inmates spent some of their day making furniture. Here they were watched over by a guard so sleepy and sluggish that Jenkin told the others that his brain only flickered into life when he sucked on his pipe.

First steps

Jenkin began on a lock he had constant access to – the one on his cell door. He measured the size of the keyhole with a stolen ruler, and worked out the rough position of the levers within the lock by placing a strip of paper within, and making impressions on it with a thin knife.

Whenever a warder locked or unlocked his cell door Jenkin made a mental note of the shape of the key, and by a process of trial and error, managed to file down his own wooden key to the correct shape. All the cell doors worked on the same key, so Jenkin was able to copy it for his fellow escapers.

Broom crank

The next lock to overcome was the steel outer door of the cell. This was far more difficult as it could only be unlocked from outside. But there was a way around the problem. Each cell had a window overlooking the corridor and the escapers managed to get to the lock by employing an ingenious cranking device, made out of a broom handle and parts made in the workshop. Another wooden key was shaped in the same painstaking way as the first, but it took four long months of trial and error to get it right.

Moumbaris kept the device in several pieces in his cell, where he assembled it when needed.

The outer door of the cell was opened by a key attached to a wooden crank and broom handle.

Inner door
Outer door

Crank

Key

Broom crank

Outer cell door

The broom handle was kept, naturally enough, attached to a broom, and the key crank was disguised as a coat hook. The key itself, the only part of the mechanism which could arouse suspicion, was hidden away.

After solving the problem of the first two locks, the escapers then set out to make keys for every other door they needed to open, or cupboard they may need to gain access to.

Impressions in soap

Some of the keys they needed were ones which were left in locks during the day. While a guard was looking the other way these could be whisked out of their locks and pressed hard into a bar of soap – leaving an impression that could then be copied at leisure.

Other locks in less obvious places could even be temporarily removed and taken apart to work out the size and shape of the key needed to open it.

Key collection

As their key collection grew they began to realize that some were very similar to ones they had made already, and would only require minor adjustments to make them work in other locks. Even better was the fact that some keys they had already copied would unlock at least one other door on the way out.

But one of the doors they had to open had no key. It was electrically operated from the main office where the night warder sat. They would have to make sure that the guard was elsewhere when this door was to be opened.

Damning evidence

After several months, so much incriminating material had been collected by Jenkin, Lee and Moumbaris that they were

Imprints of keys were made in soap.

becoming anxious that it would be discovered.

Clothes were a distinct worry. Obviously the three could not escape in their prison uniforms, so had set about collecting any civilian clothing they could find. Surprisingly, this had been quite easy. T-shirts were ordered for "sportswear", and bundles of rags for washing the floor included perfectly wearable jeans and shirts.

Jenkin's escape outfit was salvaged from rags used to clean the prison.

Shower storeroom

They were soon presented with a golden opportunity to hide their hoard. One day workmen came to repair a faulty shower heater, housed in a cupboard behind the shower room, and carelessly left this cupboard door open.

The escapers unscrewed the lock on this door, studied it to make a key, and replaced it before any guard noticed it was missing. They were then able to keep their escape equipment in this cupboard. This was especially convenient because if it was discovered, then the guards would not be able to tell who it belonged to.

Time runs out

The pressure on them to escape shortly was growing. Jenkin had managed to smuggle in enough money to pay for the initial journey away from the prison. But South Africa's currency was changing, and this money would soon be out of date.

Also, another prisoner, John Matthews, was due for release very soon. The three felt sure that if they broke out after his release, the South African authorities would try and implicate him in the escape, and possibly return him to prison. They had to go before he was set free.

Lastly, the escape clothes they had gathered together were only suitable for the summer, which was fast coming to an end. Clearly, an escape had to be mounted soon, but there were still some final details which needed to be sorted out.

Mystery locks

In their thorough preparations, almost all the forged keys had been tested in the locks they were intended for. But two keys remained untried. One was for a door in the corridor on the way to the exit, the other was for the final outer door to the prison. These would have to be tried on the night of their getaway. If they did not work, the escapers would have to resort to chisels, files and screwdrivers.

They also needed to make sure the right man was on duty on the night that they chose to go. The right man in this case was Sergeant Vermeulen – he was the most lackadaisical, inefficient guard they could think of.

Fragrant getaway

So on December 11, 1979, the final preparations for the escape were made. That afternoon, as

Hiding keys

Keys for the escape were concealed in several hiding places around a cell, for example in a box of soap powder, or jar of sugar. Some were placed in plastic bags and buried in the garden in the yard, underneath a particular plant, to help the escapers remember where they had left it.

they daydreamed about food they would soon be able to eat, and friends they would shortly be seeing again, the three tidied their cells, intending to leave no clues. If they did get out of Pretoria Prison, dogs would be sent to trail them, so they washed the clothes they had worn that day, sprayed the cell beds with deodorant, and sprinkled pepper over their prison shoes.

Plans flushed away

All secret letters and plans were flushed down the lavatory. Jenkin felt a strong sense of regret as he did this, and was surprised to realize that he was destroying items that had come to possess great sentimental value for him. Spare keys were given to a trusted cell mate to bury in the garden for any future escape. Jenkin even dyed his footwear – bright yellow running shoes – a less conspicuous shade of blue. Dummies made of prison overalls stuffed with towels, clothes and books, were placed in their cell beds. Shoes were positioned at the bottom of the beds, to look like feet.

Ready to go

Despite the preparations the day passed slowly. The escapers tried to remain as calm as possible, and the guards gave no indication that they suspected an escape was imminent. Perhaps they too were bluffing, and waiting to pounce.

At shower time the heater cupboard was opened up, and civilian clothes were placed in order for speedy dressing. A set of workshop tools was prepared – a screwdriver and chisel for stubborn locks, and a file to adjust any faulty keys.

At supper, to fortify themselves for the ordeal ahead, the three ate as much of the almost inedible prison soup as they could, and returned to their cells.

They then set out to see if the plan they had so painstakingly prepared would actually succeed. The diagram below shows what happened next.

Door C

Door B

Door A

Jenkin's cell

Lee's cell

Shower room

Moumbaris's cell

① ② ③ ④ ⑤

①

At 4:40pm Jenkin, Lee and Moumbaris unlock their inner cell grilles (door A) with forged keys. Moumbaris opens his outer cell door (B) with the broom crank, and then opens the outer doors of Jenkin and Lee's cells.

②

Escape equipment (clothing, keys and door-breaking tools) is collected from the shower room cupboard.

③

Jenkin unlocks corridor door (C) with a forged key. A fuse box on the landing wall next to this door is forced open and sabotaged, which causes all the lights to go out on the first floor.

④

Locking door C behind them, the three escapers go down the stairs to the ground floor and hide in a storage cupboard in the stairwell.

⑤

Alerted by noise from protesting prisoners, night warder Vermeulen unlocks the ground floor corridor door (D) and goes upstairs to investigate the "power failure".

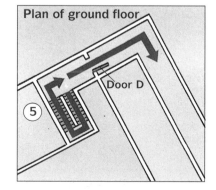

Plan of ground floor

Door D

⑤

After Vermeulen has passed them and is safely up in the first floor corridor attempting to settle complaining inmates, the three emerge from the cupboard and hurry through open door D.

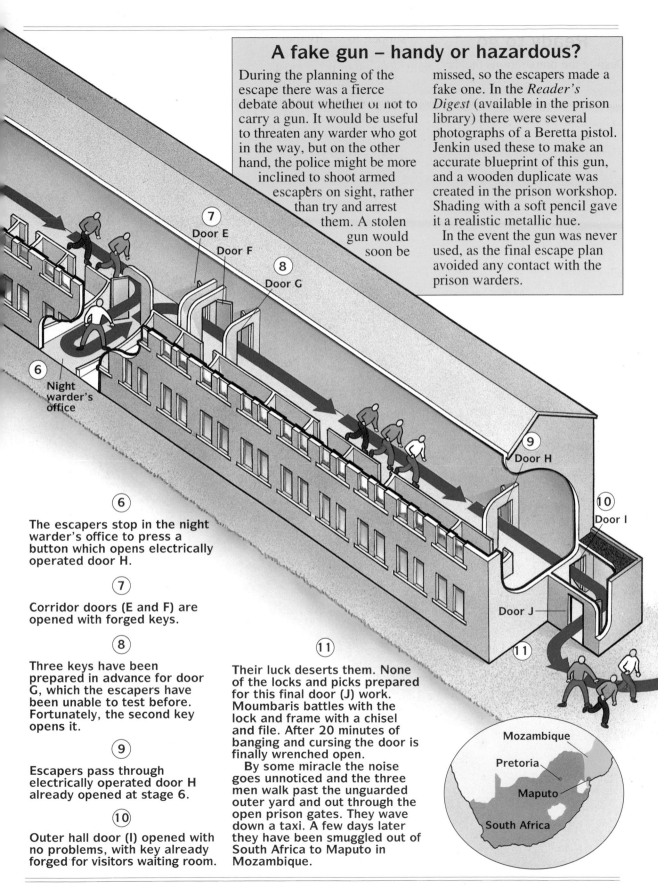

A fake gun – handy or hazardous?

During the planning of the escape there was a fierce debate about whether or not to carry a gun. It would be useful to threaten any warder who got in the way, but on the other hand, the police might be more inclined to shoot armed escapers on sight, rather than try and arrest them. A stolen gun would soon be missed, so the escapers made a fake one. In the *Reader's Digest* (available in the prison library) there were several photographs of a Beretta pistol. Jenkin used these to make an accurate blueprint of this gun, and a wooden duplicate was created in the prison workshop. Shading with a soft pencil gave it a realistic metallic hue.

In the event the gun was never used, as the final escape plan avoided any contact with the prison warders.

Door E
Door F
Door G

7
8
9 Door H
10 Door I
Door J
11
6 Night warder's office

6
The escapers stop in the night warder's office to press a button which opens electrically operated door H.

7
Corridor doors (E and F) are opened with forged keys.

8
Three keys have been prepared in advance for door G, which the escapers have been unable to test before. Fortunately, the second key opens it.

9
Escapers pass through electrically operated door H already opened at stage 6.

10
Outer hall door (I) opened with no problems, with key already forged for visitors waiting room.

11
Their luck deserts them. None of the locks and picks prepared for this final door (J) work. Moumbaris battles with the lock and frame with a chisel and file. After 20 minutes of banging and cursing the door is finally wrenched open.

By some miracle the noise goes unnoticed and the three men walk past the unguarded outer yard and out through the open prison gates. They wave down a taxi. A few days later they have been smuggled out of South Africa to Maputo in Mozambique.

Mozambique
Pretoria
Maputo
South Africa

Mountain-top escape for Italian dictator

On a July morning in 1943, commando captain Otto Skorzeny stood nervously in an outer office of "the wolf's lair", Adolf Hitler's secret headquarters in east Prussia. He had seen the German dictator before, as a distant, revered figure at huge military parades, but never met him face to face.

Hitler's friend

With great formality he was ushered into his leader's presence and promptly told some extraordinary news. Benito Mussolini, Italy's fascist leader and Hitler's friend, had been arrested by his own countrymen. Italy, Germany's closest partner in the Second World War, was on the brink of surrender. Hitler told

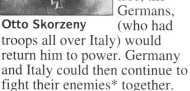

Otto Skorzeny

Skorzeny he expected him to fly to Italy and rescue Mussolini. No risk was too great. Once he was free, the Germans, (who had troops all over Italy) would return him to power. Germany and Italy could then continue to fight their enemies* together.

The most hated man in Italy

Mussolini, who had ruled Italy for 20 years, had been taken prisoner on July 25, after a meeting with the Italian King. The King told him the war seemed lost, and that he, Mussolini, was now "the most

Benito Mussolini (right). His decision to join Germany in World War Two led to his overthrow. The Italian Government tried to stop German troops from rescuing the fallen dictator by hiding him in different locations (below).

Hiding Mussolini

Corsica

③ September. Flown by seaplane to hotel in Apennine mountains.

Albergo-Rifugio.

Rome

① July. Arrested in Rome. Taken in ambulance to Ponza.

Italy

Sardinia

② August. Taken from Ponza by cruiser to Italian naval base at La Maddalena.

hated man in Italy". Soldiers bundled him into an ambulance and drove off to a secret location. The Italians knew the Germans would want to rescue Mussolini, and would stop at nothing to find him.

Message intercepted

So the hunt for Mussolini began. Over the summer he was taken to three different hiding places (see map), and it took several weeks for the Germans to track him down. Skorzeny knew Mussolini was being held by the Italian soldier General Gueli, and when a coded message from Gueli was intercepted, giving away his hiding place, the Germans prepared to attack.

A mountain prison

The Italians had hidden Mussolini and 250 guards at the hotel Albergo-Rifugio, near to Gran Sasso, the highest

peak of the Apennine mountains. It was a good hiding place. Only a mountain cable car connected it to the outside world.

It was impossible to attack the hotel from below, but too dangerous to send in parachute troops. Skorzeny decided the only way to seize it would be to take his men there in troop-carrying gliders.

A shaky start

September 12 was chosen as the day for the attack. An Italian officer, General Soleti, agreed to accompany the rescue team. His job was to order the hotel guards not to open fire.

From an airport in Rome, gliders packed with Skorzeny's commandos were towed into the air. But things immediately began to go wrong. The glider that was to guide the attack crashed on take-off, so Skorzeny himself would have to lead the way. As he was wedged into his seat by the equipment he was carrying, he had to hack a hole in the side of the glider to see where it was going.

After an hour, they were over the mountains, and the hotel came into view. The nearer they got to their landing spot, the more dangerous it looked. It was very small, sloped steeply and was covered with boulders.

Reckless landing

Recalling Hitler's orders to rescue Mussolini at all costs, Skorzeny pressed home his attack. His glider hit the ground, and cleaved its way through a rock-strewn meadow. It came to a halt only 18m (60ft) from the hotel. Five more gliders followed, although one was smashed to pieces on the mountainside.

Hurtling out of their craft, the commandos stormed into the main hotel entrance, with Soleti shouting at the astonished Italian troops, telling them not to fire. Skorzeny, pausing only to kick over an Italian radio transmitter, dashed up the main staircase. Mussolini was in the first room he entered and two stunned officers guarding him were overpowered.

Skorzeny called on the Italians to surrender. After a short pause the Italian commanding officer accepted defeat. As a white sheet was hung from a hotel window an Italian colonel presented Skorzeny with a goblet of red wine.

Mussolini (above) leaves the hotel Albergo-Rifugio, surrounded by German and Italian troops. His former jailer, General Gueli, carries his raincoat.

This pencil sketch of the rescue (left) was featured in *Signal*, a Nazi magazine sent out to all troops fighting alongside Germany.

Una información especial

La liberación de Mussolini

The Storch which rescued Mussolini. The two-man plane could land and take off in less than 180m (600ft).

Over a ravine

Mussolini still had to be whisked away from his mountain-top prison, before the alarm was raised and more Italian troops arrived to stop them. Overhead circled a tiny two-man Storch reconnaissance plane, which landed next to the hotel. Mussolini helped his rescuers clear away boulders to make a safer runway, and then he and Skorzeny squeezed into the tiny plane and it attempted a take-off.

But the Storch was perilously overloaded. Before they were in the air they lurched over the edge of a ravine, and plummeted toward the valley floor. The ground loomed up alarmingly, but luck was with them. The pilot expertly eased his craft out of its near-fatal dive, and headed for a German airfield in Rome. Skorzeny spent a bumpy flight straining to hear the dictator as he raged against his former captors.

Wolf's lair reunion

At Rome they were transferred to a larger plane and flown to Hitler's headquarters in east Prussia. Hitler himself was waiting to greet them at the airport, overjoyed to see his old ally, and impatient to seek vengeance on the soldiers and politicians who had betrayed them both.

Berlin – the prison city

Wolfgang Fuchs' fourth tunnel was his most ambitious yet. Excavated over six months in 1964, it was over 130m (140yd) long. Thirty seven people helped with the backbreaking work, risking their lives in the hot, stale air, burrowing through mud, concrete and grime.

The tunnel could collapse or flood. If it was discovered, grenades or gas bombs could be thrown into it, killing any occupant without warning. Some of the team working on it could be double-agents who would betray their fellow workers, or even kill them.

Like most secret tunnels, it passed under a guarded wall. But this wall was not a prison boundary, it separated an entire city.

Divided lives

The Berlin Wall was one of the most infamous barricades in history. From 1961 to 1989 it separated the east and west of the city.

East Berlin was controlled by a strict communist regime, while in the west, people were freer to live as they chose. Crossing from east to west was forbidden but for many, the risks were worth taking – the hope of a better life lay on the other side.

Password Tokyo

Fuchs' escape plan worked like this.

Right. An escaper scurries through Wolfgang Fuchs' tunnel, to West Berlin.
Below. A five year old boy is lowered into the tunnel by one of its builders.

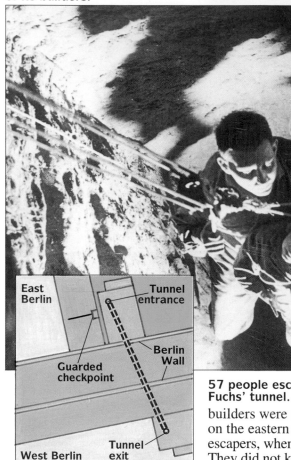

(Diagram labels: East Berlin, Tunnel entrance, Guarded checkpoint, Berlin Wall, West Berlin, Tunnel exit)

57 people escaped through Fuchs' tunnel.

On the nights of October 4 and 5, escapers arrived at 55 Strelitzer Strasse, where the tunnel entrance was located, and gave the password "Tokyo" (the host city of the Olympic Games that year). On the first night 28 people escaped – crawling for 20 minutes along the damp, airless passage to West Berlin. On the second night 29 passed through. Then things began to go wrong. Four of the tunnel builders were nervously waiting on the eastern side for more escapers, when two men arrived. They did not know the password but seemed very frightened, so the tunnellers assumed they were genuine escapers.

After a moment, the men left, saying they had to collect a friend who had lost his nerve. But they were secret policemen and returned with a soldier, announcing that all the tunnel builders were under arrest. A warning shot was fired but this turned into a full-scale gunfight, and in the crossfire the soldier was killed. The tunnellers fled back to West Berlin, but those who should have followed lost their chance of freedom.

Why was the Wall built?

When World War II ended in 1945, Germany was defeated and divided into four areas by the victors: USA, Soviet Union, Britain and France. Although the former capital, Berlin, was in the Soviet area, (East Germany) it was also divided among the four victors. However, relations between the Soviet Union and its former allies soon became very hostile.

The Soviet Union was a communist country, where the government controlled every aspect of industry, business and people's lives. The Soviets made East Germany communist too.

The other countries were democracies. Here the government has less control over industry, business and daily life, so people had more freedom.

Many people in East Germany felt they could live more exciting and rewarding lives if they moved to the

Berlin, the former capital of Germany, was deep in Soviet controlled territory.

French sector — *Berlin Wall*
British sector — *Soviet sector*
US sector — *North*
1-5km
1-3 miles

Berlin — *East Germany* — *West Germany*

west. Between 1949 and 1961 nearly a sixth of East Germany's population (2½ million people) left, mainly through Berlin.

Blockade set up

By August 1961 around 2,000 people were leaving every day. The government, worried that it was losing its most able citizens, decided to stop them from leaving.

A blockade between East and West Berlin was set up by 40,000 troops on the night of August 12-13, 1961, and the

Wall was built behind it. At first, barbed wire barricades blocked the roads, and a concrete wall was built behind them. Underground and railway train stations were padlocked shut. Barbed wire fences were also placed beneath the canals and rivers that passed between the east and west of the city. Even the sewers had heavy iron bars fitted across them.

Building the Wall

To begin with, the Berlin Wall was just barbed wire and concrete blocks, but over the next 28 years four different versions were built. Each was more efficient than the last, and so escape became more difficult. The final version was built in 1986. This diagram shows the Wall at its most complex. There were sections which were simpler.

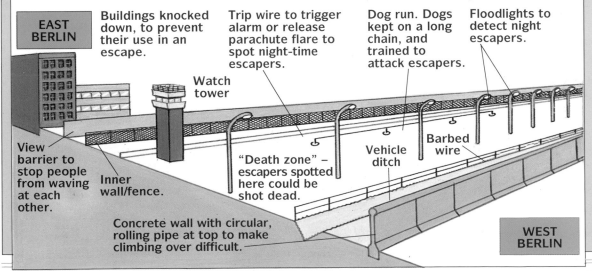

EAST BERLIN

Buildings knocked down, to prevent their use in an escape.

Trip wire to trigger alarm or release parachute flare to spot night-time escapers.

Dog run. Dogs kept on a long chain, and trained to attack escapers.

Floodlights to detect night escapers.

Watch tower

View barrier to stop people from waving at each other.

Inner wall/fence.

"Death zone" – escapers spotted here could be shot dead.

Vehicle ditch

Barbed wire

Concrete wall with circular, rolling pipe at top to make climbing over difficult.

WEST BERLIN

Fourth floor leaps and cold-blooded murder

At first, the Wall was quite easy to cross. Some houses and apartment blocks in the east overlooked the west, and people crossed by climbing out of windows in these homes. As workmen were sent to board them up, many people tried to make a hasty leap for freedom.

This led to awful scenes where escapers were pulled to and fro between East Berlin soldiers and West Berliners on the other side. As the lower floor windows were boarded up, people jumped from greater heights into blankets held by the West Berlin fire service. The first death caused by the Wall occurred in this way when 47 year old Rudolf Urban fell to his death when jumping from his apartment, a week after the Wall went up.

18 year old shot dead

In the first year over 30 people were shot dead or fatally injured trying to cross the Wall. Most of these incidents happened at night, and were usually not witnessed. However, on August 17, 1962 an 18 year old East Berliner named Peter Fechter was shot dead in broad daylight as he tried to escape. He ran toward the Wall with a friend who managed to pick his way successfully over the barbed wire. Peter was not so lucky. He was caught by a bullet as he scaled the concrete blockade. As he lay dying, West Berlin policemen could see him but were powerless to help. East German soldiers waited an hour before they fetched his body.

East German soldiers carry away the body of Peter Fechter.

West Berliners were so angered by this cold-blooded murder that they threw stones at Soviet soldiers visiting West Berlin, and demonstrations against the shooting turned into riots.

A boy leaps from a fourth floor window overlooking the Wall.

Hail of bullets halts runaway bus

Some tried to break though checkpoints in the Wall by ramming them with buses or cars. This was highly dangerous. In one desperate incident on May 12, 1963, a bus containing 12 East Berlin escapers was driven through a hail of bullets at one such checkpoint.

The driver pressed on for 100m (110yd) as his passengers threw themselves onto the floor of the vehicle. Eventually he was hit and the bus slewed into a road barrier. Most of his passengers were also injured.

Over the Wall with a luminous hammer

Many escapes would have been impossible without the help of West Berliners. East Berliner Heinz Holzapfel co-operating with friends in the west, was able to escape with his family in this way.

Holzapfel was a maintenance worker in a government building right next to the Wall, known as the "Ministeries House". Every day he went to the roof to check equipment, and up here he could peer over into the West. The idea of escape soon became irresistible.

After making careful plans he smuggled his wife and nine year old son into the building and hid them in a lavatory. When everyone had gone home they made their way up to the roof.

That night, at an agreed time, friends on the western side sabotaged the power to local Wall lights. Concealed by the dark, Holzapfel threw over a hammer which had been coated in luminous paint. Attached to it was a strong nylon rope. His friends tied a steel cable to the rope, which was then hauled up

to the roof. The cable was pulled taut and secured, and Holzapfel and his family took it in turns to slide down on chair harnesses which they had made for themselves.

Frontier guards assumed that an electrical fault had caused the lights to go out, and the escape was only discovered the next morning, when the steel cable was found draped over the Wall.

Two other people escaped in a similar way when they used a bow and arrow to shoot over a line to friends in the west.

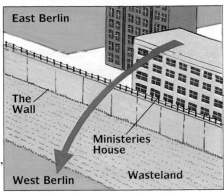

The route over the Wall.

Heinz Holzapfel demonstrates the harness his son used in the escape.

The luminous hammer could be seen clearly in the dark.

"Impossible" hiding place helps nine to freedom

Cars were a common hiding place to smuggle refugees through Wall checkpoints. At first these were in quite obvious places, such as under seats, but tighter controls were introduced and the border guards had to check each vehicle. So the hiding places became more ingenious.

In one case, an Isetta bubble car had its petrol tank removed and replaced with a smaller one, allowing just enough room for an escaper. This car was so small it was thought to be

impossible to hide anyone in it and it was exempt from the border checks. There were nine successful escapes, but on the tenth trip the Isetta's passenger shifted her position, and guards noticed the car wobbling for no apparent reason. Both driver and escaper were arrested.

The cramped journey was mercifully brief.

Isetta bubble car. The door was at the front of the vehicle.

Professional assistance – making money from the Wall

People in the west were prepared to pay professional "escape assistants" to have a family member or partner brought over from the east. These escapes were made possible by the fact that West Germans were allowed to enter East Berlin and East Germany.

Many professional escape organizations were thorough and efficient, but a few of them were callous exploiters who took their customers' money and provided little or nothing in return.

The cable reel carried four escapers.

Safe escapes (almost)

Among the best professionals were Albert Schutz, Karl-Heinz Bley, and Dietrich Jensch. One of their methods involved hiding escapers in a hollow cable reel. This was carried on the back of a truck driven over from West Berlin, pretending to be making a delivery in the east. Four people could be carried at a time. It worked perfectly on two occasions.

Unfortunately it had to be abandoned after East German

The cow had a hatch in its side.

security police blackmailed one of the escapers. They told her they would punish the family she had left behind in the east if she did not return and tell them how she had escaped.

Bley also thought up a most unlikely escape technique involving a stuffed cow bought from a theatrical shop. He fitted a reinforced compartment in the belly, just big enough to conceal one small person.

The cow was placed on the back of a truck and driven from west to east. East German frontier guards were told it was being taken to a theatre performance. The driver then picked up an escaper at an agreed location, and drove back to the west. This worked well for the first three trips, but eventually checkpoint guards became suspicious. When an East German girl named Monika Schubert was being smuggled out, the cow was examined. Schubert was discovered, and both she and the driver were arrested.

Russian disguise fools saluting guards

A few escapers succeeded by impersonating Soviet soldiers, who were allowed to travel into West Berlin. This was first tried in 1963 by a young East Berliner who made Soviet officers' uniforms for her boyfriend and two other friends. The men hid her in their car, drove to a checkpoint, and were waved through by frontier guards, who saluted respectfully.

Once news of the escape reached East Berlin, soldiers passing between east and west were inspected more carefully.

The four escapers model their fake uniforms for West German news photographers.

The guardians of the Wall

Most of the Wall guards were young East Germans on compulsory military service. Many of them did not wish to be there. Their orders were clear. Any determined escaper should pay with their life:

"If suspicious persons are in the vicinity of the border, order them to stop. If they proceed further in the direction of the demarcation line (the Wall), fire two warning shots into the air. If this step fails, shoot low to wound. If this fails, shoot to kill."

These orders gave shooting to kill as a last resort, but many escapers were killed with little or no warning. In the heat of the moment, a guard often had only one brief opportunity to shoot.

Defending the guards

Dieter Jentzen, one East German guard who escaped to the west, issued a statement defending his ex-comrades. He said that most guards were simply carrying out orders and could have killed or captured at least ten times

more escapers if they had really wanted to.

He explained that guards who made suggestions for improving Wall security, or who made many arrests were rewarded with promotion, and extra pay and leave.

An East German checkpoint guard makes a successful escape in 1961.

Soldiers who were thought to have deliberately aimed to miss an escaper were punished severely.

Jentzen begged those in the west not to taunt or despise the guards. They were in a situation over which they had no control, and were anxious for their fellow countrymen to understand this.

1,300 soldiers escape

The East German authorities knew all too well that many of their own troops were unhappy. In the two years after the Wall was built 1,300 soldiers escaped from Berlin or over the East German border. As a precaution the Wall guards were made to patrol in twos or threes, to keep watch on each other.

Pairs of guards were changed regularly to prevent friendships from forming. The atmosphere between troops was suspicious. If a soldier confided to another that he wanted to escape, he could be reported and sent to prison.

Some soldiers did overcome the atmosphere of suspicion between them. Once, two young conscripts locked another soldier they did not trust in a watchtower. With him out of the way, they were free to make a successful escape.

The Wall comes down

In 1989 the communist system collapsed in the Soviet Union and Eastern Europe. Thousands of East Germans fled from their country via Poland, Hungary and Czechoslovakia, which now had open borders with Western Europe.

In Berlin angry crowds demonstrated against the Wall, attacking it with pickaxes, and taunting patrolling guards.

The East German government decided there was no further point in preventing its citizens from escaping to the west, and the Wall checkpoints were thrown open on November 9, 1989. By the time East and West Germany

were reunited a year later, the Wall had been almost entirely demolished.

Despite the difficulties, around 5,000 East Germans succeeded in crossing the Wall before it was opened up in 1989. However, at least 172 people are known to have been killed trying to cross, and over 60,000 East Germans were sent to prison for attempting to escape.

The German magazine _Der Spiegel_ records the events of November, 1989, on its front cover.

DER SPIEGEL

DDR
DAS VOLK SIEGT
Offene Grenzen
Freie Wahlen

Escape films – fact or fantasy?

Around half of the stories in this book have featured in films which you can still see from time to time on television. While many take the true story as the basis for a more exciting, but quite fanciful adventure, others attempt to portray events as they really happened.

Hollywood's Houdini

Houdini, as a professional entertainer, made several of his own adventure films (see page 33), including *The Grim Game* (1919), *Terror Island* (1920) and *The Man From Beyond* (1921). He was tired of repeatedly performing his famous escapes and saw films as a means of reaching a large audience without having to tour.

He was also the subject of two film biographies. The first, *Houdini*, made in 1953,

Tony Curtis and Janet Leigh in *Houdini*.

was a glossy Hollywood romance. The scene shown at the bottom of the page is typical of the film's unrealistic approach. Here Houdini is chained up inside a well-secured packing case and lowered through a hole in the ice of a frozen river. Although Houdini did perform river escapes during the winter, he never attempted a trick like this under ice.

Death scene

The film ends with him dying during a performance of his Chinese Water Torture Cell trick. His actual death, from a burst appendix following an accident, was thought too unglamorous for the film. A more faithful version of his life story, *The Great Houdinis*, starring Paul Michael Glaser, was made for television in 1976.

Eastwood's Alcatraz

Clint Eastwood, as Frank Morris, makes a dummy head in *Escape from Alcatraz*.

Frank Morris's story (see pages 12-17) is portrayed in *Escape from Alcatraz*, made in 1979. It was filmed mainly on location at the island, and $500,000 was spent reconnecting electricity and decorating the prison, which had been closed for 16 years.

The director Don Siegel knew that only the actor Clint Eastwood could make the restrained character of Frank Morris interesting to an audience, and some critics rate Eastwood's depiction of the Alcatraz convict as his best ever performance.

Close to the facts

The plot sticks closely to the known facts, although many of the film's minor characters are fictitious. Most of the actors in the film became ill working in the musty environs of the prison, which gave their performances a realistic convict lethargy.

Alcatraz has been the subject of several other films, including *The Birdman of Alcatraz*, which was made in 1962 and starred Burt Lancaster.

Below. A scene from *Houdini*, showing a packing case escape from a frozen river.

Churchill's double

Winston Churchill's escape from the Boers in South Africa (see pages 10-11) and his subsequent adventures in the Boer War are featured in the 1972 film, *Young Winston*.

Simon Ward, whose resemblance to the young Churchill is striking, plays the intrepid journalist.

Devigny helps out

André Devigny's breakout from Montluc Prison (see pages 44-45) is depicted in *A Man Escaped*. To make it as accurate as possible, director Robert Bresson shot the film at Montluc and hired Devigny himself as an advisor.

The actors in *A Man Escaped* used the actual rope that Devigny made for his escape.

The lure of Devil's Island

The seediness and cruelty of the penal colony in French Guiana (see pages 4-9) captured the imagination of many film makers, and several films have been made about fictitious escapes. The most controversial was *Devil's Island*, made by Warner Brothers in 1939 and starring Boris Karloff.

Film offends

The film's harsh portrayal of life in French Guiana greatly offended the French government (who were very sensitive to criticism of the penal colony), and they retaliated by banning all Warner Brothers films from France. This cost the film company a great deal in lost ticket sales so they withdrew the film, and re-edited it to satisfy the French government.

Henri Charrière's book *Papillon*, was turned into a successful film of the same name in 1973, starring Steve McQueen and Dustin Hoffman. Although the conditions it portrays are realistic ($13 million was spent recreating the prison camps on the nearby island of Jamaica), the story, like the book, has little basis in real events.

Above. Steve McQueen plays Henri Charrière in *Papillon*. Here, while in solitary confinement, he sticks his head out of his cell to be shaved.

Below. In *Devil's Island*, Boris Karloff plays a wrongfully convicted French surgeon, who faces execution by the guillotine. In this scene he is reprieved seconds from death.

After the escape

Alcatraz Prison

(Alcatraz accordionists break out of the Rock, p.12-17)

The escape of **Frank Morris** and **John** and **Clarence Anglin** in 1962 embarrassed the Alcatraz Prison authorities. Warder Olin Blackwell had to tell newspapers that the concrete structure of the prison was crumbling away, and this had enabled the escapers to break out of their cells.

Also, by 1962 many people felt that Alcatraz had outlived its usefulness. It had been set up in the turbulent 1930s to strike fear into the hearts of American gangsters, and was now no longer necessary. So in 1963 all the inmates were shipped off the island and dispersed throughout the American penal system. Alcatraz remains open though, as a popular tourist spot, which still attracts hundreds of thousands of visitors every year.

$1 million reward

In 1993 Red & White Fleet, Inc., which ferries tourists to Alcatraz, offered a $1 million reward for the capture of the three escapers. It stated "Frank Morris, John Anglin and Clarence Anglin are excluded from this offer and are ineligible to claim the reward".

Frank Heaney, a former guard and leading authority on Alcatraz, has spoken to relatives of the Anglins, who claim to have received South American postcards from the two brothers. Frank Morris, however, has vanished without trace. Allen West, who was thwarted in his plan to escape, never regained his freedom. He died in a Florida prison in 1978.

Clarence Anglin

John William Anglin

Frank Lee Morris

These computer generated images were produced by the Fox Broadcasting Company, for the television documentary *America's Most Wanted*. They show what Morris and the Anglins could look like if they are still alive today.

Berlin Wall

(Berlin – the prison city, p.54-59)

Since the opening of the border between East and West Germany in 1989, the Wall has been slowly demolished. Whole sections have been ground down to produce gravel for building work.

Souvenir hunters or small time traders, dubbed *Mauerspechte* (Wall Woodpeckers) by the Germans, broke up parts of the Wall with hammers and chisels, and sold them on street stalls all over Europe. Now only a few sections of the Wall remain as historic landmarks.

George Blake

(Knitting needle escape for Soviet master spy, p.22-25)

Blake fled to the Soviet Union, where he was handsomely looked after by the Soviet government. He married and found work in a Moscow institute, researching politics and economics.

Sean Bourke, who helped him escape, returned to Ireland, where he wrote *The Springing of George Blake,* an account of his time with Blake. The book sold well and this encouraged him to become a full-time writer. However, this career was not a success and he died in poverty in Kilkee, County Clare, Ireland, in 1982.

Winston Churchill

(Churchill's track to fame and freedom, p.10-11)

Churchill returned to Britain to a hero's welcome, following his South African escape. He was courted by the country's leading political parties and became a Conservative Member of Parliament in 1900. He had a lifelong career in politics, becoming First Lord of the Admiralty during the First World War, and Prime Minister during the Second World War. He died in 1965.

Colditz Castle

(Colditz Castle – escape proof?, p.34-39)

Englishman **Airey Neave**, who escaped disguised as a German officer, spent 26 years as a Conservative Member of Parliament. His career ended tragically in 1979, when he was assassinated by terrorists.

His partner in the escape, Dutchman **Toni Luteyn**, remained a professional soldier in the Royal Netherlands Indies Army.

Frenchman **André Perodeau** became friends with **Willy Pöhnert**, the German electrician he had tried to impersonate. After the war Pöhnert visited Perodeau's home in Paris.

André Devigny

(Escape or death for Devigny, p.44-45)

Following his breakout from Montluc Prison, Devigny successfully escaped from France. His companion, **Gimenez**, was not so lucky. He was recaptured and his fate is unknown.

Devigny parachuted back into occupied France and carried out further undercover work with the French Resistance and the French army, during 1944 and 1945. His bravery won him many medals, including *Commandeur de la Légion d'Honneur*, and the *Croix de Guerre*. After the war he had a successful career as a soldier, and became director of physical education and sport for the French army.

French Guiana

(Snakes and sharks guard jungle prison, p.4-9)

Prisoners in the French penal colony suffered terribly during the Second World War (1939-1945), when food supplies from France virtually ceased. After the war, the French Government voted to abolish the penal settlements and bring all the remaining prisoners back to France.

Henri Charrière (Papillon) found fame and wealth when his books about life in the French penal colony, *Papillon*

and *Banco,* became best sellers. Royalties from the film *Papillon* added to his fortune. He settled in Spain, but died in 1973, only five years after *Papillon* was published. (See film section, p.60-61, and *Further Reading,* p.64).

Eugene Dieudonné returned to Paris, following his official pardon in 1929. He remarried his wife (they divorced when he was deported), and returned to his former trade as a cabinet-maker.

Harry Houdini

(Harry Houdini – escaping for a living, p.30-33)

Both Houdini and his wife **Beth** were fascinated with the supernatural and spirit world. Before his untimely death in 1926, Houdini had promised Beth that if he died before her, he would do everything he could to contact her from beyond the grave.

For the next ten years Beth held a seance (a ceremony where people try to make contact with the dead) on the anniversary of his death, but no message came, and she gave up trying to reach him.

David James

(Ivan Bagerov – Royal Bulgarian Navy, p.18-21)

After the war David James became an Antarctic explorer, and was a Conservative Member of Parliament between 1959-64 and 1970-79.

Benito Mussolini

(Mountain-top escape for Italian dictator, p.52-53)

Following his escape from the Apennine mountains, Mussolini became leader of a fascist republic in northern Italy, which fought alongside Germany. He was captured by

Italian guerrillas in April 1945, and executed.

German commando **Otto Skorzeny**, who rescued him from the Gran Sasso, survived the war and was tried as a war criminal, but charges against him were dismissed. He moved to Spain, where he became involved in the ODESSA organization, smuggling former Nazis to South America, where they would not be prosecuted for their war crimes.

Gunter Plüschow

(Plüschow's dockland disguise, p.26-29)

Plüschow's successful escape won him an Iron Cross medal, personally presented by Kaiser Wilhelm II. He survived the First World War to write about his adventure in the book *My Escape from Donington Hall*. (See *Further Reading*, p.64.)

Pretoria Prison

(Breakout at Pretoria Prison, p.46-51)

Tim Jenkin returned to South Africa in 1991 and now lives in Johannesburg, where he works as a press officer for the African National Congress. **Stephen Lee** lives in London where he works as an electrician for a national newspaper. **Alex Moumbaris** lives in Paris where he works in the computer industry.

Harriet Tubman

(Harriet "Moses" Tubman leads slaves to freedom, p.40-43)

Harriet Tubman spent the years following the abolition of slavery looking after her parents in a small house she had built in Auburn in New York State. She was buried there when she died, aged 93. Her tombstone states "She never ran her train off the track and never lost a passenger".

Further Reading

Berlin then and now by Tony Le Tissier (Battle of Britain Prints International Ltd, 1992)

Camera in Colditz by Ron Baybutt (Hodder and Stoughton, 1982)

Devil's Island – Colony of the Damned by Alexander Miles (Ten Speed Press, 1988)

Escape from Alcatraz by J. Campbell Bruce (Futura Publications Ltd, 1979)

Escape from Montluc by André Devigny (Dennis Dobson, 1957)

Escape from Pretoria by Tim Jenkin (Kliptown Books Ltd, 1987)

Escaper's Progress by David James (Corgi Books, 1978)

Inside the Walls of Alcatraz by Frank Heaney and Gay Machado (1987)

My Escape from Donington Hall by Gunter Plüschow (John Lane, The Bodley Head Ltd, 1922)

Papillon by Henri Charrière (Granada Publishing Ltd, 1980)

The Life and Many Deaths of Harry Houdini by Ruth Brandon (Secker & Warburg, 1993)

Acknowledgements and photo credits

The publishers would like to thank the following for their help and advice: Hans-Juergen Dyck, Haus am Checkpoint Charlie, Berlin. Frank Heaney, Red and White Fleet, Inc., San Francisco. Tim Jenkin, Johannesburg. Dr. David Killingray, Goldsmiths College, University of London. Micheline and Gérard Laruelle, La Châtre. Sidney H. Radner, Houdini Historical Center, Wisconsin. Mark Seaman, Imperial War Museum, London. Marina Tchejina, St. Petersburg.

The publishers would also like to thank the following for permission to reproduce their photographs in this book: Associated Press, London (4, bottom; 13, top right; 56, top right); Centre d' Historie de la Résistance et de la Déportation, Lyon (44); Cincinnati Art Museum, Subscription Purchase/Charles T. Webber (43); Daily Express, London (22, bottom); Der Spiegel/Spiegel-Verlag, Hamburg (59, bottom); Fox Broadcasting Company (62); Golden Gate National Recreation Area, San Francisco, USA (14 middle; D. Denevi, cover, middle; 12, top; 14 left; Richard Frear, 17, bottom; Charles R. McKinnon, cover, bottom right; 17 middle); Haus am Checkpoint Charlie, Berlin (54; 56, top left, bottom; 57; 58; 59, top); Hulton Deutsch, London (5, top right, bottom left; 10; 22, top; 23; 24; 28, right; 29, right; 32, middle; 52, top; 53; 61, top left); Hulton Deutsch/Bettman Archive (31); Imperial War Museum, London (34; 35; 36; 38); Peter Jenkin © Tim Jenkin (49); The Kobal Collection, London (60; 61); Leicestershire Museums, Arts and Records Service, Leicester, UK (26; 29, middle); Mary Evans Picture Library (28, middle); Pacific Aerial Surveys, Oakland, USA (cover, top left; 13, middle); Peter Newark's Western Americana, Bath (40, top and bottom; 41, middle); Courtesty of the Sidney H. Radner Collection, Houdini Historical Center, Appleton, WI, USA (30, bottom right; 32, bottom left; 33); Robert Hunt Library (52, middle); H. Roger-Viollet © Collection Viollet, Paris (3; 4, top right, middle; 6; 7; 8); H. Roger-Viollet © Harlingue-Viollet, Paris (5, bottom right); Eli Weinberg © Tim Jenkin (46, top).

The tradename Vaseline is used with permission of Chesebrough-Ponds. Illustrations on page 29 are used with permission of Unilever History Archive (Vaseline jar) and Sarah Lee H & PC (Kiwi polish). The illustration on page 45 is used with permission of Thiers-Issard.

The publishers would also like to acknowledge the following for the use of the film stills on pages 60-61: Columbia/Open Road/Hugh French (Carl Foreman); Papillon Partnership/Corona/General Production Co./Robert Dortmann; Paramount (George Pal); Paramount/Malpaso (Don Siegel); Warner (Brian Foy).

Index

Berlin Wall, 54-59, 62

escape techniques
  boat, 7, 8, 9, 29
  disguise, 18-21, 29, 34, 38-39, 49, 58
  dummy, 14-15, 17, 36, 49
  glider, 37, 52-53
  hole in wall, 14-15, 37
  rope and ladder, 23, 35, 44-45, 57
  tunnel, 35, 54
escape tools 3, 15, 17, 23, 36-37
  fake gun, 51
  fake identity card, 18, 23, 36
  fake keys, 47, 48

getaway vehicles, 23, 25, 56, 57
guards, 6, 46, 49, 59, 62

Houdini, Harry, 30-33, 60, 63

lock picking, 31, 44, 47

prison colony, 4-9, 61, 63
prison security, 12, 27, 34, 46
prisoner of war camps and prisons ,
  Alcatraz, 12-17, 60, 62
  Colditz, 34-39, 62
  Donington Hall, 26-29
  Marlag, 18-21
  Montluc, 44-45
  Pretoria, 46-51
  Wormwood Scrubs, 22-25
prisoners, famous,
  Blake, George, 22-25, 62
  Charrière, Henri *Papillon*, 6-7, 63
  Churchill, Winston, 10-11, 61, 62
  Capone, Al, 13
  Mussolini, Benito, 52-53, 63

slavery, 40-43, 63
solitary confinement, 6-7

World War One escapes, 26-29
World War Two escapes, 18-21, 34-39, 44-45, 52-53